BACKCOUNTRY

BACKCOUNTRY

JENNY GOEBEL

SCHOLASTIC INC.

Copyright © 2023 by Jenny Goebel

All rights reserved. Published by Scholastic Inc., *Publishers since 1920.* SCHOLASTIC and associated logos are trademarks and/or registered trademarks of Scholastic Inc.

The publisher does not have any control over and does not assume any responsibility for author or third-party websites or their content.

This book is a work of fiction. Names, characters, places, and incidents are either the product of the author's imagination or are used fictitiously, and any resemblance to actual persons, living or dead, business establishments, events, or locales is entirely coincidental.

ISBN 978-1-338-85788-7

10 9 8 7 6 5 4 3 2 1   23 24 25 26 27

Printed in the U.S.A.   40

First printing 2023

Book design by Maithili Joshi

FOR COURTNEY, THANK YOU FOR BEING MY FRIEND
FOR ALL SEASONS

IN THE DEPTH OF WINTER, I FINALLY LEARNED THAT
INSIDE ME THERE LAY AN INVINCIBLE SUMMER.

ALBERT CAMUS

CHAPTER 1

The day everything changed, I was playing in a regional volleyball tournament. The gym's fluorescent lights seemed harsher than usual. The buzz of the crowd, which I normally found energizing, was having the opposite effect. Each yell and cheer seemed to drill into my head and drain my stamina away. As we huddled up, I felt the pressure mounting. I was the starting outside hitter. Our team's entire offensive strategy was structured around me, the lead attacker. My teammates were counting on me to bring us to victory in the third and final game of the match. Win this match, and the tournament was ours. The problem was my stomach was off. The inside of my mouth felt like it had been rubbed dry with a cotton rag, and as slowly as my legs were moving, you'd think my kneepads were made of lead.

"Coach, I need a minute," I said. I didn't give her a chance to respond before making a beeline for where my parents were sitting in the bleachers.

Dad spoke first, and he sounded a little aggravated. "What's going on, Em? Why aren't you with your team?"

"I don't feel good," I said.

Mom immediately placed a hand to my forehead. "You do feel a little warm."

"Of course she does," Dad said. "She's been working up a sweat out there."

My parents glared at each other. No doubt, Dad didn't like the way Mom was babying me, and Mom didn't like the tone of Dad's voice. A groan of regret slipped through my lips. Why had I said anything? Dropping dead on the court might've been preferable to getting caught in the cross fire of one of their spats.

But, judging by the way their scowls quickly transformed into looks of concern, it seemed my groan was mistaken for one of physical discomfort. I didn't correct them, because it very easily could have been, the way I was feeling.

"Maybe you should sit the last game out," Mom suggested. And there it was again—another comment I knew would get under Dad's skin.

My eyes flicked to his face. Sure enough, the vein in his neck popped out and his cheeks turned a light shade of red. He'd played some college basketball before a knee injury ended his career. As much as he liked to talk about it—the comebacks, the buzzer shots—you'd think his baller days had taken up a quarter of his life instead of a few short years.

One thing was certain, he hadn't missed a single minute of playing time by choice. I could only imagine how disappointed he'd be if I asked to sit out the championship match. My stomach roiled and I shifted my weight from one foot to the other. I really did feel awful, but Dad had torn himself away from work to be here. I didn't want to let him down, and I didn't want him to leave if he decided it wasn't worth his time to be here.

"Sports aren't everything," Mom said almost pleadingly as she brushed Dad's forearm with her fingers. The three of us knew that Dad didn't share her opinion. Even if he wouldn't come right out and say it, sports meant the world to him. He'd given up interest in practically every other aspect of my life.

When Dad's business took off, he'd started drifting away, and it wasn't until I started playing competitive sports that he'd made any real time for me.

I was glad he never missed any of my games, but we used to enjoy just hanging out together. Anyway, he only seemed to care about how I performed on the court. That was one reason I was so excited for the cross-country ski trip we planned to take over winter break. Out in the wilderness, I knew I could remind him that my skills went beyond what I could do in a gym. This trip was the first time he was going to take me into the backcountry for more than a day. While we were off the grid for close to a week, I wouldn't have to compete with his real estate clients for his attention. I wanted to show him that I wasn't just sporty. That I was also strong and adventurous and tons of fun to be around.

Dad had bristled at Mom's touch and the reminder, but he softened when he spoke to me. "Think you can fight through?" he asked.

I weighed my options. If I went back on the court, it would make him glad that he'd rearranged his schedule to be here. If I sat out, he'd be counting the potential income he'd lost by canceling an open house so he could watch my matches. Still, I couldn't remember the last time I'd felt so rotten. My head felt wonky, I thought I might puke, and my energy was completely zapped. If I said no, I knew he wouldn't make me play. But if I said yes, I'd make him proud. He thought I was a fighter, and ultimately, I couldn't stand the idea of that changing.

I nodded at last. "Yeah, I think I'm just a little dehydrated," I said. "Can I have another Gatorade?"

"Atta girl," Dad said at the same time Mom dug into the small cooler she'd packed for the tournament.

"This is the last one." She held out a bottle of Riptide Rush. "How many have you had?"

I snatched the drink from her hands and shrugged. "I don't know," I said. "I lost count." Then I took off before Mom had a chance to fuss over me some more. Which I knew would only set off another round of endless irritability between my parents. Just thinking about it worsened my stomachache.

I could see the relief in Coach Vega's eyes as I returned to the sideline. My teammates had drifted apart and were scattered around the bench. Ignoring their curious glances, I lifted the Gatorade to my lips, tipped my head back, and drained the bottle dry.

"You okay?" Coach asked when I'd finished chugging.

"Yeah," I said. I wasn't, but I forced a smile anyway, hoping she'd find it convincing.

"Impalers, circle up!" she yelled. We'd decided on our team name during the first practice, when Deanna failed to dig one of my spikes. She said it stung so bad where it struck her that it was like being impaled. Once everyone had gathered around, we stacked our hands together before swinging them upward. "Bump, set, impale!" we all shouted.

I knew we needed something to get us fired up, and normally, I'd be the one encouraging my teammates and boosting morale. But I was just too exhausted. I could hardly lift my arms into the ready position. There was no way I could raise anyone else's spirit when mine was so low.

It was a struggle to focus. I tried to keep my eye on the ball as it volleyed around the court, but my head was in a fog. Every time I ran, it felt like I was trudging through mud. Still, I somehow managed to score a few key points, keeping victory within reach. I wanted the win so bad; I could practically taste it.

Ayra's pass from the back row fell right into Brooke's outstretched fingers. She cradled the volleyball for a split second before returning it to the air. It was a perfect set, high and close to the net. This was it. I clenched my teeth and began my approach. I wanted to crush the ball. I craved the rush of adrenaline and power that I'd felt countless times when spiking the ball onto the opponent's court.

But . . .

My feet barely left the ground. My swing was weak and after meeting my hand, the ball formed a high, slow arc. It hung in the air so long my best friend Tanner's three-year-old sister could've kept it from landing on their side of the court. As it was, a girl in the back row easily slid her forearms beneath the ball and bumped it to the player closest to the net. The setter returned the ball to the air, and seconds later their outside hitter sent it careening back in my direction. The seconds ticked off like minutes. I was filled with dread when I saw how, unlike my spike, her hit was sharp and exact. I mustered what little energy I had left and dove forward with my arms outstretched. All I had to do was get there before the ball did—something that normally wasn't that difficult for me. But with the game on the line, I didn't have it. I came up about a mile short, and just like that, it was over.

While I peeled myself off the floor, my eyes landed on Dad. My heart sank when I saw the disappointment in his face. I wanted to fall back onto the court and disappear into the cracks between the maple planks. But somehow, I stumbled to my feet and walked toward the sideline.

Coach Vega huddled the team together. There was an awkward silence, and I could feel everyone's eyes on me. Stunned. They all looked stunned. The championship should've been ours. It *would* have been ours if I hadn't blown it for everyone. I thought my stomachache couldn't get any worse, but it did. Not only did I feel nauseous, but now it felt like a knot was tied in the middle of it. The Impalers would never say it out loud, but I knew they'd been counting on me, and I'd let them all down.

Eventually, Coach snapped back into it. She pushed a smile onto her face and faked cheerfulness as she mumbled something about it "being a close one," and that we'd "come out on top next time."

7

I went through the motions. The faces of the other team's players blurred together as we walked into two opposing lines and slapped hands. Then they screamed, and celebrated, and collected the first-place trophy.

Dad was gone by the time Coach released us to our parents. Mom said he had to get back to work. The thing was, I knew he would've stuck around to congratulate me if my team had won. My shoulders drooped farther, and Mom wrapped an arm around me. "Like pouring salt in a wound," she said. Her voice was mostly sympathetic, but it was laced with a rage I knew wasn't meant for me.

"At least he came," I said. I don't know why I felt the need to jump to Dad's defense, but I did. I also didn't know exactly what salt in a wound felt like, having never experienced it, but I knew it meant making a bad situation even worse. That was accurate.

Mom waited until we were on the road to ask, "Are you feeling any better?" She was doing that thing where she pretended her eyes were totally on traffic, while really, she kept glancing sideways at me. Being an only child, I got to be the star of the family. But I also got Mom's undivided concern, and she tended to worry about everything.

"Yeah," I lied. I didn't have the energy to talk about how crummy I felt. And I didn't know how much of it was physical discomfort and how much was disappointment.

I'd used the restroom before we left the gym, but I had to go again already. "Can you drive a little faster?" I asked.

Mom pressed her lips and exhaled loudly through her nose. If she hadn't known before, she knew now that I hadn't been telling the truth. She didn't call me on it, though, and instead stepped on the gas.

Once we got home, I hit the bathroom, after which I filled a water bottle and then melted into Dad's recliner. No matter how much I drank, I was still parched. And my head felt too heavy for my neck to support. *I must be coming down with the flu. I just need some rest and then I'll be okay.* Even as I was thinking it, I knew it wasn't true.

Mom asked a question, but it sounded like gibberish to me.

"Hmmm?" I mumbled. "What?"

She came close. She looked into my eyes while worrying her lip and fussing with my hair. "Are you achy?" she asked as she pressed her hand against my cheek. "Is your throat sore?"

I shook my head, which caused a wave of vertigo to wash over me. "Dizzy," I said wheezily.

"Something's not right." Her voice sounded constricted, like she was the one having trouble breathing. "I'm calling an ambulance."

"No. I'll be okay," I said, but Mom was dialing 911 before the breathy words finished leaving my mouth. She had rushed me to the ER once for a chipped tooth. And with the way she reacted to me having something as small and insignificant as a splinter, I guess it wasn't a surprise that she was freaking out now. Dad took a calmer approach to, well, everything, but he wasn't here.

Maybe I'd sponged up some of Mom's anxiety. Or maybe whatever was wrong with me caused my heart rate to go berserk. Either way, my chest was thrumming wildly by the time the ambulance arrived.

A man wearing a dark blue uniform and a stony expression strode into our living room. He came directly to my side. While he cuffed my arm and took my blood pressure, he exchanged words with my mom. I couldn't follow their conversation, but what I did understand was that nothing he said erased the fear splashed across Mom's face.

Whatever was happening to me, I sensed from this moment on, my life would never be the same.

That wasn't something I wanted.

Sure, I wanted *some* things to change. I wanted my parents to get along better. I wanted to see Dad more than just when he came to my games. I wanted another shot at winning the tournament, and I wanted to get rid of all the pink in my bedroom and decorate in grays and teals instead.

But I was aware enough to know that I wasn't holding a winning lottery ticket. My life wasn't changing for the better, and I wished more than anything that I could do something to hit the brakes. Sameness was safe. It was comfortable.

"You're going to feel a prick." Before I could register the paramedic's words, something sharp pierced the tip of my ring finger.

"Ouch," I cried. The sting wasn't that bad, but I hated needles.

The paramedic frowned. He and Mom exchanged more words. They spoke to me, too, but beyond my head feeling fuzzy, I was totally maxed out. Nothing sank in.

I could barely keep up with the flutter of activity around me. The unhurried air about the paramedic seemed at odds with how quickly he accomplished his tasks. Next thing I knew, I was being rolled out our front door. Fear engulfed me as I took in my changing surroundings—the gurney I was lying on, the medical equipment, the chill of the night air followed by the confinement of the ambulance. When I felt the rumble of the engine starting and then the jostle of the road, I began to understand just how rapidly things were changing, and *sameness* felt like the most desirable thing in the world.

Mom sat on the bench behind the paramedic. The expression on her face had gone from fearful to stricken, and that did nothing to silence the alarm bells going off in my head. My gaze trailed downward to the smear of brilliant red blood on my recently pricked finger before shooting back to the paramedic. I'm sure he saw a mixture of fear and confusion in my eyes. I'm sure it was a look he got a lot. "When I tested your blood sugar levels, they were dangerously high," he said. "You're being transported to the hospital for further evaluation."

It was easier to track what he was saying than it had been a minute before, but I still struggled to make sense of his words.

"Diabetes." Mom filled in the blanks as she fought to keep her voice steady. "We think you have type 1 diabetes."

CHAPTER 2

A few weeks later, I was back at school and standing next to my locker. Tanner's eyes bored into me as I considered eating the small bag of pretzels he was offering. He had to think it was weird that I was leaving him hanging. We'd always shared snacks after school. But that was before I had to think about the number of carbohydrates in my food, or how long it had been since I last tested.

A feeling like I'd just stepped off a roller coaster hadn't left me since my official diagnosis. With every doctor's appointment and adjustment to my daily routine, I felt a bit wobblier and more nauseated. Yet I didn't know if it was my body letting me down, now that I knew I had diabetes, or if I was grieving over everything that I thought I'd lost. I craved a return to normalcy. As if it was somehow possible.

"I'm not hungry," I said at last. "Thanks, though."

"I didn't think . . . I mean . . . I'm sorry," he said. So we both knew I was lying.

"Don't be," I mumbled. He hadn't done anything wrong, and it wasn't that I couldn't eat pretzels anymore. I just didn't want to deal with any of it right now. It had been a long day, and it was far from over. Instead of the pretzels, I would grab a snack at home when Mom could help me calculate the insulin I'd need before my volleyball game that night.

"Yeah," Tanner said a little gruffly. "See ya." Then he walked away.

I sighed. I'd only spent a few days in the hospital. Time seemed to stand still while I was there, but when I returned to my life, I felt completely out of step with everything and everyone. My schoolwork and practices were the same as before, but now I also had to balance my food intake, test my levels frequently, and visit the school nurse during lunch and passing periods. I knew Tanner wanted to help and was hurt that I wasn't letting him. But it was kinda like when you're holding a bazillion things and someone offers to help you carry the load, and you know that if they pull something from your arms, everything will come crashing down.

I didn't have long to dwell on the latest moment of awkwardness between me and my best friend. Despite Mom's misgivings, she'd finally given in to my protests and agreed to let me play in another tournament with my team. As soon as Tanner walked away, I hurried out of the school building to where Mom was waiting in her car to pick me up. We swung by home, and as I rushed around to get ready, she asked, "Are you sure you want to play tonight? You could just wait until tomorrow, when you're fresh."

"I'm sure," I said.

"It's okay to pull back on some things. In fact, I've been meaning to talk to you about the trip . . . Your dad could cancel now and get a full refund for the huts. You could go next winter instead . . ."

I couldn't believe she was doing this to me now. Well, actually, I could. Mom had leveled up to "professional worrier" in the past few weeks. "Mom, please," I said. "I need food, and I don't want to be late." My team was counting on me, and Dad was meeting us at the gym. We didn't have time to question tonight's plan, let alone a trip that was months in the future. Plus, I was dragging enough without letting Mom's worries pull me further down.

She grimaced, then nodded. I could tell the small smile that followed was purely for my benefit. Still, she seemed in a somewhat agreeable mood, so I handed over the kit containing my testing strips, monitor, and insulin pens.

She hesitated for a split second before taking them from me. "Okay, but you've really got to start doing this yourself one of these days."

It wasn't that I didn't know how. I'd been thoroughly

schooled on managing my diabetes before ever leaving the hospital. Mom and Dad and Dr. Morlock kept reminding me that most kids my age administered their own shots. But most kids my age didn't have a serious needle phobia.

I chose to ignore her comment and instead said, "Thanks, Mom."

Coach Vega subbed Sarah in for me five minutes into the first match when it became clear to everyone that Mom was right. I wasn't ready for a triumphant comeback.

I always play best when I don't have to think about every move I make on the court. When my mind and body work together seamlessly, I am pure action. Even though my sugar levels were in range during the match and I felt fine, I just couldn't get my head there—into the zone or whatever you want to call it. Right before Coach pulled me, I whiffed on a spike. It was humiliating.

As I slumped off to the sideline, I avoided Dad's eyes. The view from the bench wasn't something I was used to. I watched my teammates' shoes skid across the floor. I stared at the kneepads stretched tight around their legs. The Impalers looked good, but not good enough. The other team was racking up points and there was nothing I could do about it.

I wanted to give it my all. I wanted to rebound the way Dad

and Dr. Morlock had claimed was possible, but "my all" just wasn't what it used to be. My ability was still there, but I was mentally exhausted from all the changes to my life. I'd lost my focus, and without it, my teammates couldn't depend on me.

The worst part was that Coach Vega wasn't even going to register the Impalers for this tournament. We were a last-minute entry after Dad convinced her that I needed a chance to "get back on the horse" rather than waiting for the next season to begin. And since Dad's company, Walker Realty, was a major sponsor of our team, it wasn't like she could say no.

So here we were. I'd failed miserably at "overcoming adversity," and my team was suffering through another painful loss because of me. I winced when Sarah missed a block and the ball slammed down on our side of the court, racking up yet another point for the opposing team. Coach Vega gripped her clipboard tightly, obviously resisting the urge to throw it.

"Put me back in," I said, but I knew I didn't sound as though I believed in myself. So why would she? Sure enough, when she searched my face, her eyes betrayed her lack of confidence.

"Maybe next game," she said.

Ouch.

I took a sip of Gatorade to hide my embarrassment.

"Doesn't that have a ton of sugar?" Ellie squirmed on the bench next to me.

The entire team had heard about my trip to the hospital. "Yeah," I said stiffly, "so?"

"I mean, my aunt has diabetes and Dad said it's because she ate so much junk food her whole life. I just thought—"

Just then the other team missed Sarah's serve and the Impalers scored their first point. I jumped to my feet to celebrate, grateful that the interruption allowed me to ignore Ellie's comment. I knew she didn't mean anything by it, but it stung. It made it sound like my illness was somehow my fault. Like I could've prevented it if I'd only made better choices. That wasn't true. My doctor said people confused type 1 diabetes and type 2 diabetes all the time. But even type 2 wasn't caused solely by an unhealthy lifestyle. Genes played a big role.

Ellie's comment continued to needle me while I watched the game slip away from our team. And it wasn't just the game; pieces of my life were being torn away, and I couldn't do anything to stop it. I was far from being a star player today. Would I ever be one again? Nothing seemed to make Dad prouder than when I was scoring points and winning matches. Would he keep coming to my games just to watch me sit on the bench? No way. My stomach felt like I was the one who'd been impaled by a volleyball and all the wind had been knocked out of me. Maybe I was overreacting, but I worried that the biggest loss to come from all of this wouldn't be my consistency on the court or in championships or anything else. The biggest loss would be the last shred of interest my dad still had in me and my life.

Things went from bad to worse after we were the first team to be eliminated from the tournament. As we slowly started to disperse, Coach caught up with Dad and me. "Mr. Walker," she said, "I know this probably isn't the best time, but did you receive my email about the fundraising for next year? There are going to be some wonderful opportunities to showcase our girls' abilities to top-tier college scouts. The team will have to travel a bit more, however, and you've always been such a huge supporter . . . I know this is a bit forward, but if you could only commit to matching what you donated this season . . ."

Dad cast her the same fixed smile from the photo that appeared on all his marketing materials. His website, flyers, business cards, even a bench at the busiest bus stop in town displayed him smiling, well dressed, and strolling through a green space while touting, "Buying a home with Walker Realty really is a walk in the park."

In reality, my dad never "walked" through any park. Jogged or sprinted, maybe.

He quickly glanced in my direction. His Adam's apple bobbed, the way it always did when he was put on the spot. "I think we're going to have to take a wait-and-see approach on that," he said meaningfully.

"Oh," Coach Vega replied. "Oh, I see. Of course, I just thought . . . You know what, we've got time. Why don't I just reach out after the holidays?" She furtively gave me a once-over, and I could tell she was trying to assess my current condition. Considering I'd wound up in the hospital after the last tournament, I guess her concern made sense. It wasn't like she'd be able to tell, though, if I did need medical attention. Most of the time, I looked and felt completely normal.

I'd typically bristle at being treated like a science experiment, but right now, my annoyance couldn't compare to the nausea my dad's answer had unleashed. If he was questioning whether he wanted to sponsor the team, did that mean he was questioning my future as an Impaler? It was one thing to worry about him not coming if I sat on the bench. If he thought I couldn't even be on a competitive team now, I was really in trouble. What else was he having doubts about? Was our winter cross-country ski trip in jeopardy? I thought Mom was the only one doubting whether I would be up to it. I needed Dad on my side or the trip really would be canceled.

"Sounds good," Dad said to Coach, and then started walking again.

I couldn't walk. Not in my current state of alarm. My chest felt tight, and it was hard to breathe. I'd been looking forward to the trip for ages. Not only was I desperate to get into the beauty and stillness of the backcountry after the mess my life had become, I needed quality time with my dad. How else was I going to keep him from slipping out of my life completely?

When Dad realized I hadn't fallen into step behind him, he stopped and turned. "You all right, Em? You look pale. You did check your glucose after the game, right?"

"Uh-huh," I said. My blood sugar levels were fine. It was apprehension that glued my feet to the floor this time. I'd been focused on all the other changes to my life since my trip to the ER. But I'd believed Dr. Morlock when he said I could still play sports. That I could still do all the things I'd done before. What if I couldn't? Or what if I could do everything I had before, just never at the same level? It could cost me more than a starting position for the Impalers. My dad only paid attention to my life when I was winning tournaments and trophies. If that all stopped, and I couldn't reel him back in while we were in the backcountry, I really could lose him for good.

"I was just thinking about our trip. I can't wait," I said, and forced a smile.

"Okay," Dad said evenly. "That's still a long way off." Was I imagining it, or had he used his negotiator's voice with me? He slipped into this tone when he was talking about real estate and didn't want to give anything away. If he sounded too cheery, it could make the sellers seem desperate. Too brusque and the buyers might be scared off. If he was using this tone to talk to me about the trip, it meant backing out had been on his mind. He just didn't want me to know it.

"Right. I'll be back to myself by then, for sure," I blurted, hoping my enthusiasm sounded convincing instead of anxiety ridden.

Dad wrapped his arm around my shoulder, and we started walking out of the gym together. "That's the spirit," he said. Still, I sensed that he was holding back. There wasn't the pure delight in his embrace that was normally there after a big win. Even with his arm around me, I could already feel the added distance growing between us.

CHAPTER 3

The one good thing to come from the early elimination from the tournament was that, instead of having matches all day, my Saturday was now wide open. And for once, there was something I was more excited about than playing volleyball.

While Mom was getting my insulin shot ready before breakfast, I said, "Can we visit Top Dog today?" She probably wished I'd waited to ask until she was done calculating the dosage, but I liked having something to distract myself while the needle was piercing my skin.

I flinched when I felt the prick, but I cheered right up when Mom said, "I don't see why not. I have a few things to take care of around the house this morning, but then we can go."

Dad was sitting next to us at the table, scrolling across his phone screen and sipping his coffee. He'd been planning to spend the day at the tournament, so I thought this might actually be a fun thing for us to all do together. "Can you come, too?" I asked hopefully.

His eyes flicked to me and then back to his phone. "Sorry, Em. I've got some fires to put out at the office. A house didn't appraise well, and the buyer is getting cold feet."

"Oh, okay," I said. Seemed like there was always some sort of emergency. If it wasn't a bad appraisal, it was a bad inspection. It was strange how those things could wait if I had a game but not when something else came up that was just as, if not more, important to me.

My endocrinologist was the one who told us about Top Dog, at my appointment the week before. He'd bombarded us with information on my chronic illness. So much that it made my head swim. However, I'd paid close attention when Dr. Morlock started talking about a local company that trained diabetic alert dogs.

The dogs were specially trained to respond to low blood sugar levels. They could literally smell a drop as it was happening. As if I needed more proof that this experience was really freaking Mom out—it took hardly any convincing to make her see I needed one. In fact, she was the one who persuaded Dad to buy a Top Dog. They were really expensive, but if we went somewhere more affordable, I might have to wait a year or more. We'd contacted them immediately after the appointment and had already started the process. In addition to diabetic alert dogs, Top Dog trained guide dogs, hearing dogs, mobility assistance dogs, seizure alert dogs, and psychiatric service dogs. I'd been matched with a black Labrador retriever named Molly. I couldn't bring her home yet, but I could visit her while she was in training. I just wished Dad would be there when I met her for the first time.

"It'll be nice to have another dog around here," Dad said. I think he was trying to make up for bailing on us. When he glanced up from his phone again, and saw my face still reflected the disappointment I was feeling, he added, "I used to bring Champ into the backcountry with me. Maybe your new alert dog can come with us on our trip."

I couldn't help it then. My face broke into a grin, and I said, "Awesome!" at the same time Mom stiffened. Probably for multiple reasons. She hadn't warmed any to the idea of me going on the hut-to-hut adventure. Plus, she'd resisted the idea of getting another dog ever since Champ passed away. Champ was the golden retriever my parents got shortly after they were married. He'd died of old age when I was five.

Whenever I talked about wanting another dog, Mom would say the same exact thing: "We're too busy. Puppies are a lot of work. We don't have time to train one." Dad had trained Champ, but that was long before his brokerage took off and we started seeing less and less of him.

The fact that the diabetic alert dogs came fully trained

probably made it easier for her to say yes, but I suspect she would've said yes to anything that might play a role in saving my life. Maybe she was having second thoughts now. I wasn't, though. I was beside myself about finally having a four-legged companion again. Even better, it sounded like unless Mom threw up a roadblock (which was a good possibility), the trip was still on!

An hour later, I was in the back seat of Mom's car, and Tanner was sitting beside me. Mom had asked my best friend (via his mom) to go with us after Dad opted out. I should've been happy about it, but she'd called Mrs. Nowak without consulting me first. It was the first time since my life had been turned upside down that I'd seen Tanner outside of school. It was awkward enough when we had a few minutes together in a noisy hallway. It was extra uncomfortable riding next to each other in near silence. Especially since my mom was keeping tabs on us through the rearview mirror as she drove.

"How are you feeling?" Tanner asked quietly. We hadn't really talked about what I was going through. I wasn't comfortable enough with my diagnosis to share all the details with him yet, and I think he sensed that, because he seemed nervous. Not sure how to answer at first, I took in his appearance. He'd changed his hairstyle recently. It had been shaggy for as long as I could remember. Now it was short on the sides and back, and curly on top. It made him look older. I liked it, but I didn't tell him that.

"Fine," I said at last. Then I stared at my lap. It wasn't like I was going to lay it all out in the open now. I wanted to focus on happy things. Between my volleyball career going up in flames and my new life revolving around needles and testing strips, I wasn't ready to rehash all my recent disappointments. Not even with Tanner.

We usually talked so much when Mom was driving us somewhere that I forgot she was there. Most likely, she tuned us out, too. Now I could feel her hanging on every word I spoke, trying to get a read on me. It was probably why she'd invited Tanner along in the first place. She was worried about me and wanted me to settle into my "new normal."

"So you're finally getting a dog," Tanner said. "That's cool."

"Yep," I said. "I mean, I won't actually get the dog for a while still. She, um, has to go through more training." I glanced at the cooler in the front seat. The one containing a sample of saliva Mom had collected when my blood sugar was low. It was required for my future alert dog to get acquainted with the scent. We'd already turned in several samples of my saliva, but we brought another with us to save on overnight shipping expenses.

I hardly wanted to talk to my best friend about the unique smell of my spit. Maybe it would've been fine a few years ago, back when I never got nervous around him. But then he went and started running his fingers through his hair and holding my gaze when he cast me a dimpled smile after I'd made a free throw. And, I don't know, I guess I didn't want to gross him out. I also liked that he'd always been impressed by my speed and the way I handled myself on any court. I didn't want him to know how much I was struggling. How I worried about the way everything was suddenly changing. So I did something I rarely did: I shut him out. For the entire car ride, I barely talked at all.

Still, by the time we reached Top Dog, I was bursting with anxious energy. I couldn't wait to meet Molly! I sprang from my seat the moment the car was parked. The brick building didn't look like anything special—a lone structure in a dirt lot surrounded by fenced-in areas—but somewhere beyond the glass front doors, my future twenty-four seven companion awaited!

I was so excited that I forgot Tanner and I were no longer little children. I blurted, "Race you there!" and took off sprinting across the gravel. I could sense Tanner on my heels, but it wasn't until I crossed the finish line that I realized he'd been dogging it the entire time. My best friend had never purposely let me win at anything before. He was as fierce a competitor as I was. A deep-down part of me crumbled. Was it because he thought we were too old to be racing, or was he holding back because I'd been sick? Couldn't he see that I was every bit as fast as I'd always been?

I brushed off my annoyance and looked to Mom, who hadn't taken a single hurried step. She was only halfway across the lot. "Mom, please?" I begged, while bouncing on my feet a little. She smiled in return and quickened her pace.

Tanner and I let her enter the glass doors first. While the man at the front desk greeted us, I peered around him, hoping to catch a glimpse of Molly. But I could only see to the end of a long hallway, and there were no dogs in sight.

"What's the name?" the man asked.

Mom nudged me softly. "Emily," I said. "Emily Walker. I'm here to see Molly." He was infuriatingly calm as he slowly typed something into his computer and scanned the screen. How could he not see what a monumental moment this was? It warranted at least a tad more enthusiasm on his end.

"Ah, there we go," he said, and picked up a receiver. "Hey, Heather, can you bring the black Lab in D-Group up front? She has a visitor."

I held my breath as I peered down the hallway. A few eternal moments later, a young woman and a Labrador retriever stepped into view. The dog wasn't puppy size, but she gave off a puppy vibe with her springy gait.

I'm not exaggerating when I say it was love at first sight.

When Molly's big brown eyes met mine, and her tail started to wag, everything that had happened leading up to that moment melted away. It didn't matter that my return to volleyball was an epic failure, or that things were weird with Tanner, or that Dad was possibly pulling his sponsorship, or that I'd recently been thrown the biggest curveball of my life. All that mattered was my joy right then and there, and for a second, I knew what it was like to feel invincible again. As quickly as the rush came, it was gone. But now I knew I was still capable of feeling triumphant.

Looking into Molly's eyes, I felt brave and not nearly so alone. She was exactly the boost I needed at exactly the right time. I silently made a vow that nothing would stop me from going on the ski trip with Dad. I would show him how much fight I had left in me. He would renew his sponsorship for the Impalers and maybe, just maybe, I would get my old life back.

CHAPTER 4

I couldn't hold on to my optimism every moment of every day for the next three months, but somehow, I managed to keep Mom from canceling the trip altogether. Then, just one day before it started, I was worried that's exactly what she had in mind. As I dug through the bottom drawer of my dresser, searching for enough base layers to last a week, Mom stood just inside the doorway to my room. She'd perfected the art of hovering long before my diagnosis. "What about sugar cubes? I know they're not on the list, but you might need some. You never know what could happen."

I exhaled loudly as I slid the drawer shut. Sugar cubes were not on the list because I'd packed plenty of glucose tablets. If I tried to pack every little thing I *might* need, I'd never make it out the door. Which was likely what she wanted. "Why don't you just say it?"

"Say what?"

"That you don't want me to go on this trip with Dad."

She drifted closer. She brushed my arm with her fingers. "It's not that I don't want you to go, Em. But maybe it's too

31

soon. Maybe you need more time . . . Maybe we all need more time to adjust before you go off somewhere so remote. If something goes wrong . . ."

Was it too soon? Would I ever feel ready? Doubt started closing in on me, but there was more than just this trip at stake. Not that I was surprised by it, but since volleyball season had ended, Dad had worked every single weekend. He'd even stopped coming to my appointments with Dr. Morlock. I knew what his answer would be when Coach Vega contacted him after the holidays. If I was going to resurrect my volleyball dreams and save my relationship with Dad, I had one week to change his mind.

I shifted my eyes away from Mom and busied myself with rummaging through another drawer. "Do you think three pairs of wool socks will be enough?"

"I'm serious. I shouldn't have to tell you what could happen if your blood sugar goes too high or too low again. If you skip a meal, or . . ."

I stopped packing and stood up. Molly raised her head. She'd been resting on the carpet beside my bed and was trained to stay with me all hours of the day. One thing hadn't wavered these past few months—the love I'd felt ever since I first laid eyes on her. I'd visited her every Saturday for two months while she continued her training and then, about a month ago, she'd come to live with me for good. When I only straightened to my full height instead of taking a step, she relaxed, like she was supposed to, and I returned my attention to Mom.

I'd always towered over all my friends. In the last year, I'd really shot up. Dad says to use whatever leverage you have—in sports, and in life. If you're faster or taller than your opponent, make sure they know it. At thirteen, I was at least two inches taller than my mom. "I'll be fine," I said. What I didn't say was how much I needed this trip. I hadn't wanted to be right the night I rode in the ambulance. But the truth was, everything had changed. Not only in ways that could be measured—like all the finger pricks and insulin doses and, yes, blood sugar levels—but every single relationship I had was different as well.

My relationship with Mom had changed the least. She'd always been a worrier, concerned with every bump, bruise, or sprain. My diabetes just made her extra anxious. The changes in my relationships with my teammates and friends, and with my dad, bothered me more. Take Tanner: The incident at Top Dog, when he'd let me win the race, hadn't been a one-off. Ever since, whenever we shot hoops in his backyard, he treated me like I was fragile or something. He'd had no problems going full charge into a layup and wiping me out before. But now, even though he'd never admit it, I could tell he was taking it easy on me. And I hated it.

I hated it even more that, when Dad was home and happened to glance in my direction, it seemed like he mostly saw wasted potential. For as long as I could remember, I'd been athletic. After I'd failed at "getting back in the saddle," the way Dad hoped I would, things hadn't improved. When I needed a burst of energy, it wasn't always possible.

I didn't know who I was if I wasn't an athlete. Dad might've been taking it even harder than I was, though. His acting so dejected was strange considering he prided himself on having an indomitable spirit. Not that we ever talked about what was going on in his head. Mom said his side of the family never talked about anything important. Sports, weather, entertainment, yes—but try to bring up emotions, relationships, anything meaningful really, and they'd just clam up.

I hoped that wouldn't be the case on our trip. Dad and I would be spending five days of winter break deep in the Rocky Mountains. We'd be trekking through the snowy wilderness by day and finding warmth and rest in a different hut each night. Other than Molly, we'd only have each other for company.

Back in the spring, when Dad first presented the idea, it

had been for all three of us to go. Mom had immediately backed out, saying she wasn't up for all the cold. She didn't love the outdoors the way Dad and I did. And for the past three months, she hadn't stopped pushing Dad to cancel the entire thing, or at least leave me at home.

"Dr. Morlock said I could go," I reminded Mom. The thing was, Dad and Dr. Morlock were a lot alike. They were both "you can do anything you set your mind to" type people. Dad had searched for a diabetes specialist with a background in sports medicine as soon as I'd left the hospital. I knew Dr. Morlock wouldn't have been Mom's first choice. I wasn't certain how much she valued his opinion. Still, he was a specialist.

Mom shifted her feet. "Doctors can be wrong."

I felt my resolve hardening. Mom didn't understand, but I couldn't back out the way she had. Not only did I need to prove to myself that I was up to the challenge, but I also wanted Tanner to see I was still the same girl who eliminated him at almost every game of knockout we played. If I was capable of this, maybe the Impalers would think it was possible for me to come back stronger next season. Most of all, I needed to show Dad that I was still the champion he'd always been so proud of. How would I ever believe in myself if he didn't believe in me enough to sponsor the team I was on?

"Four people with type 1 diabetes have climbed Everest. And the number one cross-country skier in the U.S. has diabetes and has competed in the Olympics four times," I said, repeating what Dr. Morlock had told me. "Were all their doctors wrong, too?"

The frown lines on Mom's face deepened. I could tell she didn't like what I was saying but didn't know how to respond.

I took her moment of hesitation to add, "If I can learn to manage my diabetes in the wilderness, I can deal with it anywhere. Plus, I'll have Molly to keep an eye on me." The black Labrador retriever perked up again at the sound of her name. She'd been trained to be a diabetic alert dog for nearly two years before she came into my life—ever since she was a puppy, and long before I was diagnosed. The saliva I provided helped further her training. She'd been taught how to sniff out changes in my blood sugar levels. Now she could detect whether my levels were going too high or two low before even my meter could. She knew when and how to paw my leg, wake me if I was asleep, or go alert one of my parents if I wasn't responsive.

She was the best thing that had happened to me in months, if not years.

There was a subtle change to Mom's expression. "Molly is wonderful, and I know how much you love her. Just remember

36

that she's still learning, too, and she can't detect a problem one hundred percent of the time." Mom leaned forward and encircled my body with her arms, half hugging, half caging me in. "Please be careful," she whispered in my ear. "I almost lost you once already."

CHAPTER 5

Mom was quiet the next morning while we transferred my clothing and diabetic supplies into backpacks. She re-counted my injection pens, making sure I had triple what I should need, and then divided them between two insulated storage packs.

"Don't let these get too cold," Mom warned. "Or too hot, but I can't imagine that being an issue."

She was treating me like a five-year-old, but I managed to hold back an eye roll. "Okay," I said. The whole packing thing was a balancing act of keeping our bags light enough to comfortably ski through the backcountry while making sure we had all the essentials. In addition to our food and clothing requirements, we had a long list of general equipment and emergency items to lug along. I felt bad that Dad kept adding more and more of the items to his bag so I wouldn't have to carry so much. When it was all divided up, I had one storage pack of insulin, half the glucose tablets, my testing kit, a water bottle with its own insulated carrier, trail food (aka fast-acting carbs), a few odds and ends, and what I'd be wearing on the trail—hat, boots, gloves, that sort of thing. Molly would wear her own saddlebag that identified her as a service dog and held a few additional emergency items. Dad had everything else.

Mom trailed behind us as we tossed our packs in the shell of Dad's truck. The brown winter grass we stood on was covered by frost. The thin layer of ice wouldn't last long, though, considering the way the rising sun was making it glisten. The snow in the mountains was another story. It would likely last all winter.

Dad caught me staring at the jagged, white-capped peaks on the horizon. "We got lucky," he said. "It's going to be a bluebird day."

I smiled faintly, then opened the cab door for Molly before hopping into the front seat of the truck. A bluebird day was a cloudless day. A day full of hope and happiness under a sky the color of the bluest jay. A bluebird day was a day full of promise. And yet my stomach felt tied in knots. A back-country adventure could go wrong a hundred different ways for anyone. For me, it presented additional challenges. It didn't matter how badly I wanted to go, or that I'd been skiing practically since I could walk. I was afraid I wasn't up to it, and that we'd have to cut the trip short because of me. If that happened, it was a safe bet competitive volleyball would be over as well.

Mom leaned in through the open door to give me one last hug. She'd hugged me three times already that morning— once immediately after I'd walked out of my bedroom, once after giving me my first injection of the day, and once after breakfast. She still smelled like the cinnamon raisin oatmeal we'd eaten. I didn't want a long drawn-out goodbye. I didn't want to dwell on how lonely and worried she'd be all week. I swiftly squeezed back, then reached for the handle to pull the door shut between us.

She walked around to the driver's side and gave Dad another run-through of warning signs and dosage amounts. He should've known already, but since he'd missed so many of my appointments and had hardly been around lately, he probably needed the refresher. She reminded him that we didn't know yet how my body would react to prolonged exposure to the cold. That was the thing about managing my diabetes. It was a moving target. There were patterns, but nothing was ever certain.

The longer Mom lectured Dad, the more I shrank in my seat. This was exactly why I needed to get away. I knew my diabetes was a twenty-four seven thing. I could never escape it, but I longed to go somewhere where it didn't feel like the center of everything.

Mom eventually ran out of instructions, and Dad and I were finally on our way. As we passed where Tanner lives three houses down, I felt a familiar pull. I'd learned in one of the survival classes I'd taken with Dad that humans have a tiny amount of magnetic material in the bone between their eyes. Some scientists think it's like an internal compass that helps people "sense" true north. It didn't seem to me that there was a compass behind my nose, but it did feel like there was one in my heart sometimes, pulling me toward the people I cared about.

As if she could sense my yearnings, Molly poked her dark, wet nose through the crevice between the door and the seat. I scratched behind her right ear. She wagged her tail in response, nearly whacking Dad in the face, and then she curled up on the back seat of the cab.

I turned my attention outside the window again. As early as it was on the first day of winter break, I knew Tanner would be sleeping. I sighed, wishing I'd gotten up the nerve to go see him or text him the night before. But I'd been afraid I'd get the same reaction from him that I had from Mom. Hesitation. Doubt. Concern. I couldn't risk having those kinds of emotions rub off on me as I faced a new challenge.

I twisted the bright orange paracord bracelet on my wrist. Tanner had made it for me years ago and I'd forgotten about it until I was packing. It wasn't the same as talking to him, but having it with me made me feel a tiny bit better.

When Molly stuck her right paw through the crevice, I

knew exactly what she was trying to tell me, even though she couldn't reach my leg. "Thanks, girl," I said before popping a glucose tablet in my mouth. Dad glanced in my direction, but he didn't say anything. Instead, he piped alternative music from his phone through his truck speakers. The lyrics of every song on his playlist seemed to be some sort of variation of "live life to the fullest." Don't give up. Don't look back. Don't give in to fear. There were so many mixed messages in the world. Mom always wanted me to "be careful and play it safe." Dad wanted me to "go for it." They couldn't both be right, could they? I didn't know if I was being brave by going on this adventure or really stupid.

We drove for hours, barely talking, and little by little we escaped the city. Tall buildings, rows of houses, and heavy traffic gave way to peaks and valleys, trees and winding roads. Sure enough, the sky was a brilliant blue. But after the previous night's snowfall, it looked like someone had come through with a spoon and left dollops of whipped cream on all the evergreen branches. Except, snow is heavier than cream, and some of the branches were bowed. Some looked on the verge of breaking. They needed the sun, I thought, the same way I needed this trip—to melt away what was weighing them down. The branches and I both needed our loads to be lightened so we could spring back to the way things were before the storm.

CHAPTER 6

The trailhead looked like nothing more than a pullout on the side of the highway. The unpaved area had been cleared, but walls of muddy snow surrounded the small lot. The truck chugged off the asphalt, bounced on the uneven ground, and rolled into a spot. Dad grinned at me before popping open his door. A blast of frigid air swept into the warm cab. It smelled like car exhaust, a hint of pine, and a whiff of new beginning.

I swung open my own door and was about to plop myself onto the frozen ground when Dad came around the back side of the truck bed. "Whoa there. Aren't you forgetting something?"

I'd promised Mom that I'd test my levels as soon as we arrived. Dad was holding me to it. Apparently, I couldn't even leave the truck first. I glanced at Molly for support, but she only gave me a look that made me think she was on Dad's side.

"Fine," I said. I pulled out my kit—gauze, a testing strip, monitor, and lancet (aka needle)—and got to work. It had been two hours since I'd eaten. After a tiny amount of blood-shedding, I was happy to see that the number displayed was well within the normal range. Since I was about to exercise, though, I opened a box of mini raisins and dumped the entire thing in my mouth.

"Awesome," Dad said. "Now we get to have some fun." The grin on his face told me this was Dad at his best. As Mom would say, "He was really in his element." He wasn't moping, he was optimistic, and now I'd have to do my part to keep him this way.

Molly barked and wagged her tail, seemingly as eager as Dad was to hit the trail.

I wouldn't call the gearing-up part "fun." By the time we'd wiggled into enough warm, water-resistant layers of clothing, strapped on our packs (including Molly's), laced up our boots, grabbed our poles, climbed to higher ground, skinned up our skis, and then clicked in, I was exhausted.

"You doing okay, Em?" Dad asked.

"Never better," I said with a slight twinge of annoyance—more at myself than with Dad. We weren't ten minutes into this adventure, and already I was coming off as weak. To prove a point, I dug in my poles and launched myself forward. "Just try to keep up," I said as I glided through the heavy snow. The skins were smooth going one direction and grippy

44

going the other. That way, I had traction going uphill, but I wouldn't slide backward.

Molly shot after me, clearly enjoying herself as she ran in my tracks, and Dad responded to my sudden burst of speed with "That's my girl." I felt a swell of pride. At one time, Dad had hopes of me making the U.S. Ski Team. But then other sports had crowded it out. Competitive leagues took over my life and I'd had fewer and fewer weekend days to trek to the mountains with Dad. I hadn't missed the skiing as much as I'd missed just being outdoors.

Most of the trails I'd skied before had been groomed—certainly the downhill skiing I'd done at the big resorts. The snow on this trail was all fresh and untouched—no tracks, only powder. Because it wasn't compacted, it was more difficult to shuffle through, and my pack felt cumbersome on my back. The speed I'd started with just wasn't maintainable. But like with any sport, I knew the beginning would be a struggle. There was always this period before my blood got pumping when everything was extra hard and tiring.

Even though we both knew Molly could keep blazing the trail, she stayed close to my side. It wasn't long, though, before my muscles warmed up and I fell into a steady stride. Dad took up the rear. Then it was just the scenery, not the exertion, that was taking my breath away as I glided through

the wintery landscape. The trees, the rocks, the underbrush—
everything appeared to be coated in a layer of sugary white
frosting. That had been one of my biggest fears when I found
out I had diabetes—that I'd never be able to lick whipped
frosting off another cupcake, eat a chocolate chip cookie, or
even down a soft drink. I thought being diabetic meant no
sugar. Ever.

Luckily, that wasn't the case. I could still have sugar, like
anyone else, as long as I didn't go overboard, and had other
healthier foods along with it. In fact, sometimes sugar was my
friend. If I was having a hypo, where my blood sugar went
too low, a sugar cube or jelly beans might be exactly what I
needed to get my levels back to where they needed to be.

I stepped and slid, stepped and slid, and Molly followed
in my wake. It appeared easier for her to stay in the tracks my
skis made than plod along in the powdery drifts. Everything
was so quiet. So peaceful. Even the thoughts in my head fell
silent. I hadn't experienced anything near calm in so long.
For months, my thoughts had been piercing and relentless.
They'd planted seeds of doubt and worry and insecurity. But
breathing in the crisp, clean air, feeling the softness of snow
beneath my skis, and seeing nothing but endless beauty, my
head felt clear. I felt strong and alive. I felt well, and that was
huge for me.

"Emily!" Dad's voice rang out, breaking the spell I'd been under. I was surprised that he sounded so far away. I stopped in my tracks and Molly came to a halt behind me. When I glanced over my shoulder, I didn't see him anywhere.

"Dad?" I called back. A second later I caught a flash of his red ski jacket in the forest behind me. When he fully emerged from the trees, he didn't look happy. That confused me. I thought things were going great. I felt good. It had turned out to be a bluebird day, just as he'd predicted. I didn't know what had happened to sour his mood.

"You can't do that, Em," he said as he glided up to me.

What had I done? I thought he'd be proud of how I'd overcome the heavy snow. We were traveling at a slight incline, and I'd worked hard to cover as much ground as we had already. It would take us four to five hours to ski the seven or so miles to the first hut where we'd be hunkering down for the night. A steady pace was important, and I'd kept to it.

"You missed a trail blaze."

My stomach dropped. "Really?" I asked. I thought I'd been following the trail. The trees were sparser on the route I'd taken. But I'd lost myself in the splendor of my surroundings. I couldn't say that I'd kept a close watch for markings on the trees.

"We were supposed to take a right turn a while back," Dad continued. "Two triangles forming a right diagonal painted on the trunk of a tree. Remember?"

I nodded. I remembered what the trail sign meant. I didn't remember seeing one.

"And—"

I grimaced. "There's an 'and'?"

"*And*, I had to stop to check on a binding and you had no idea. You left me behind. We *cannot* get separated out here."

Dad was right. He was carrying the trail map, compass, and altimeter, along with the bulk of our supplies. He had what we both needed to survive. What concerned me more was how seriously he was taking what I thought was a forgivable mistake. The look on his face was stern, and I thought I even saw fear in his eyes.

That stopped me cold. If this had been a year ago, Dad would've jokingly called me a "speed demon" or something for losing him. If he reprimanded me at all, it would've been slight. Instead, it looked like he was already having regrets about bringing me on this trip, and I absolutely couldn't have that.

"It won't happen again," I assured him. Then I held my breath while Molly, sensing my discomfort, leaned against my leg. Even through my ski pants, I could feel her warmth.

Dad scrutinized me for another moment. "Okay," he said at last. Then he turned around and started back the way we'd come.

I exhaled. I knew I'd gotten off easy. At the very least, Mom would've scolded me if she'd been here. Most likely, she would've made us turn around and go home. As I slid my skis along the trail we'd forged, I thought maybe I deserved one of Mom's lectures. It hadn't been difficult for Dad to follow Molly's and my tracks and find us, because it was a bright and windless day. We could backtrack now and return to the trail. But if our tracks had been covered or we'd traveled too far in the wrong direction, it could've been disastrous.

This trip was meant to be fun. And so far, it had been—fun and peaceful and rejuvenating. But I'd let myself get lulled into thinking that I was somewhere safe, and that was not okay. Even more was at stake than Dad's attention and my future as an Impaler. Because no matter how magnificent nature seemed, I couldn't forget that it could also be cruel and unforgiving. Underestimating the outdoors could be deadly, especially for me.

CHAPTER 7

Hours later, I was still disappointed in myself for missing the trail marker, and I couldn't seem to shake it. The wintery landscape was every bit as beautiful, but it seemed to have lost some of its sheen. Even Molly burying her nose in the powder, then tossing snowflakes in the air as she lifted her snout and shook her head, couldn't lift the foul mood that had come over me.

It's funny how when you're down, you start to notice things that didn't bother you before. The sock bunched up in my boot, the way the straps on my pack cut into my shoulder blades—the real reason they were bugging me was because I was kicking myself for not being more prepared.

Dad had kept the topographic maps sprawled out on the table for the past few weeks, but he never had time to go over them with me. I'd wanted to learn the route, but the squiggly lines had been too much for me to make sense of on my own. I should've asked for help, but I didn't want him to think I couldn't handle map reading in addition to my other new struggles.

He'd added a new app on his phone that allowed him to track our route via GPS even when it was offline. But the maps were still important in case his phone battery went dead or something else went wrong.

The one thing Dad had made time for was a cross-country skiing day trip to practice, but it had been to a different location—a dog-friendly resort that was closer to home. Dad said it was to test out the equipment. I don't know if that was the real reason, or if he'd wanted to see if I was still up to the physical demands of cross-country skiing before we set out on a longer trip. I think he'd also had some concerns about how Molly would do keeping up with us in the snow.

That day, just like today, I'd started out by taking the lead. Molly had risen to the challenge as well. So much so that Dad and I joked about her being a sled dog in a former life. And we practiced navigation, but the trail had been so well traveled that it hadn't really been necessary to keep an eye out for trail markers or track our progress with maps and a GPS system. Still, if I hadn't proven that I was up to spending an entire day on skis, I wouldn't be here right now. Dad had thought then that I could do this, and I could.

I ignored the weight of my pack, and I wiggled my foot into a more comfortable position inside my boot. Molly brushed up against me, and I let my fingers trail through her silky fur. "It's all right," I said, regaining a shred of my confidence. "We've got this."

Up ahead, Dad turned and, at first, I thought he'd heard me speaking to Molly. Instead, he tapped his middle finger to his thumb. It looked silly with his gloves on, like he was a crab tapping pincers together. Really, I knew he was giving me the hand signal Mom came up with to remind me to check my levels. Within a week of my release from the hospital, Mom said she was sick of sounding like a broken record. And the finger tapping was less annoying than a verbal reminder for both of us.

I'd been sipping water from the hose on my hydration pack and munching on a variety of trail food since we set out. Still, before I could note that my mouth was dry and I'd started to feel a little sluggish, Molly was beside me, pawing at my leg. I might've pretended I didn't see Dad's hand sign, but Molly's warning was one I couldn't ignore.

My meter was stashed in an inside pocket where my body heat would keep it warm. It was a bigger hassle than usual, but within a few minutes, I'd removed my gloves, retrieved the meter, pricked my finger, and gotten a reading. Sure enough, my number was high. Dr. Morlock said the combination of cold and strenuous activity could have this effect. We'd also be eating lunch soon, and that might make my levels go even higher.

Because I have type 1 diabetes, my pancreas doesn't make insulin on its own, and insulin is needed to control the amount of glucose in my bloodstream. In other words, it was time for me to get another shot.

Dad helped me calculate the right amount of insulin and ready the injection pen. We'd been able to remain standing while I checked my levels, but now, it only made sense to take off our skis. There wasn't anything to sit on, so we got as comfortable as possible on a snowbank. I had to dig through a few layers to get to my stomach, all while trying to bare the minimum amount of skin necessary. Still, the second it was exposed to the frosty air, I gasped. I couldn't help it.

Dad made a low rumbling noise in his throat. "Problem?" he asked.

"No," I said quickly, worried I'd disappointed him yet again.

Mom always pinched my skin in a way that made the shot not hurt quite as bad, but Dad didn't have as much experience. I tried not to react again, but he still seemed to notice me grimacing.

He turned his head and inhaled through his nose. Already, it seemed like he was regretting bringing me along.

When it was over, we had to remove the needle and safely store it in a container, return the insulin pen to the insulated storage pack so it wouldn't freeze, and then double-check that we hadn't lost any of the supplies in the snow.

I still felt off, and I knew it would be at least twenty minutes until the insulin took effect.

I slipped my gloves back on, swallowed hard, and then my voice came out just above a whisper. "I think we should stay here until I have to retest."

Surprise registered in Dad's eyes. Had he forgotten that I'd need to check my levels again after a shot? He recovered quickly. "Right. Good idea." It was more than a good idea; it was really important. It was also inconvenient. And since the trip was already off to a rocky start, I felt extra bad about it.

No doubt, Dad was doing his best to be patient. But I knew how he liked to keep a brisk pace. And, honestly, I did, too. I'd always been fast. I wasn't used to making other people wait for me. The minutes ticked by slowly.

After a while, Molly began sniffing around beneath a pine tree a short distance from where we were sitting. The needles and branches were so dense that under them a patch of rich brown earth had remained unblanketed by snow.

"Something must have bedded down there last night,"

Dad commented. "Deer, maybe, or elk, seeking shelter from the storm."

Whatever it was, it had Molly entranced. And since she wasn't all that interested in me right then, it gave me hope that my levels were getting back in the normal range. That and the fact I no longer felt the need to curl up and hibernate for the winter. I guess just recognizing this meant I was learning to pay attention to my body and understanding how diabetes affected it.

Dad kept checking the time on his phone while we waited, and when it was time to retest, I pulled the necessary items back out of my kit.

"I bet you're anxious to transition to a CGM device and pump," he said.

I shrugged as I removed my gloves. I couldn't tell if he thought I should be anxious, or if, really, *he* was anxious because when I made the switch, managing my diabetes would be faster and simpler. I wouldn't hold him up so much, the way I was now, and he wouldn't have to help with the injections, either.

The CGM, or continuous glucose monitor, would be attached to the back of my arm and swapped out every few weeks. It would transmit my glucose numbers to my phone, instead of me having to prick my finger all the time to get a reading. Then a pump would be attached to my skin with a safe adhesive, and it could be programmed to deliver the insulin I needed without all the pens and needles. I'd still have to exchange the pump for a new one every three days. But overall, it was a much smaller time commitment.

Dr. Morlock wanted me to wait, though. He wanted me to gain the knowledge and experience to manage my blood sugar levels with pinpricks and an insulin pen first in case I was ever in a situation where the technology failed. "As technology is prone to do," Dr. Morlock had added. "Especially in extreme temperatures."

"Even if I already had a pump," I said to Dad, "I still would've needed my meter and pens as a backup for this trip. The devices might not work as well in the cold, or the batteries might die, and then I'd really be in trouble."

Dad would know this already if he'd been coming to my appointments, but he'd been too busy to make all but the first few. "Right, right, of course," he said. I knew Mom had tried to fill him in, but I wondered how much of the information had sunk in.

My face might've betrayed my frustration with Dad, except at that moment, Molly gave up on whatever fabulous scent she'd been obsessing over and came careening back toward us. When her front legs caught in a drift that was deeper than she'd bargained for, her back legs kept going. The result was a somersaulting ball of black fur. Within seconds, though, Molly was back on her feet, tail wagging and eyes bright as she carried on and closed the distance between us.

I chuckled before returning to my thoughts about what the future held in store for me. The thing was, I was kind of glad Dr. Morlock thought I should wait until after this trip to get a pump. On one hand, I was sick of all the strips and needles. On the other, I wasn't sure how I felt about having small devices continuously attached to my skin.

Sure, I knew I'd never be free of diabetes. I gazed at the kit I held in my hand. It was weird to be so attached to something and at the same time have such negative feelings about it. I couldn't go anywhere without it.

When I lifted my eyes, I noticed how the sun had disappeared behind the only cloud in the sky. The temperature drop was immediate, and I shivered. It reminded me that life was unpredictable. It was full of ups and downs. Still, there were moments when I could forget it all. There were moments, like I'd had this morning when I'd been as captivated by the wintery world around me as Molly was by the scent of whatever animal had lain beneath the tree.

In those moments, I felt like the old me—like the person

I'd been before my life became more difficult and complicated. What if . . . what if those moments were no longer possible after I started wearing the lifesaving devices? When needles and finger pricks were a smaller part of my life, would I feel more or less free? If the CGM and pump became a constant reminder of my diabetes, I didn't know if they'd be worth it. Not if they meant I was no longer able to forget that it was always there and never going away.

CHAPTER 8

After the numbers on my meter confirmed that the insulin had done its job, I packed up my supplies and stepped into the bindings on my skis. "Molly, come!" I hollered. I couldn't help but smile as she bounded by my side, tail wagging and tongue spilling out of her mouth. She was in heaven as she pushed through the deep snow and sidled up next to my leg. "Good girl," I said. Beyond helping me monitor my diabetes, Molly brightened every moment of my day. I couldn't imagine how I'd ever managed without her.

Once Dad double-checked our position on his GPS map and we started moving again, I felt tons better. I was free to swish through the powder and enjoy the day, as long as I kept sipping on the hose from my hydration pack and munching on the appropriate carbs now and then.

Not long after we set out again, I fell back into a steady stride. It was certainly easier letting Dad blaze the trail. Only a few times did I feel he might be dogging it so he wouldn't tire me out. I'm not gonna lie, it *was* exhausting. All uphill. My socks were bunching up in my boots again, and I was pretty sure I'd have a blister on my big toe. Leg muscles that I hadn't used in a while were really starting to ache.

Even though it was hard work and I knew I'd be sore later, it was fantastic. And I could tell Dad had gotten over how I'd slowed us down, not once but twice. He now seemed impressed that I'd kept going and hadn't complained about any of it. Every so often, he'd glance back over his shoulder and call out, "Do you need a break?" Then he'd smile softly in a way that made me feel about ten feet tall when I said no.

In fact, I felt encouraged enough to feel Dad out about sponsoring the Impalers. It hadn't come up for almost three months, but I knew Coach Vega would be emailing him soon. "Dad," I started, "you know, the regular season for my competitive volleyball team starts in January."

"Uh-huh," he replied. His voice gave away nothing.

I sped up until we were nearly side by side, so it was easier to talk. "Have you heard from Coach Vega yet?"

"Nope."

He wasn't going to make this easy for me. "It's just, I know it could be a really great season and I want what's best for my teammates, and your support means a lot to the Impalers."

Dad exhaled loudly and stopped skiing. "Look, there's a lot of stuff we need to figure out after New Year's, but let's just enjoy where we're at now, okay? Let's not spoil this trip by looking ahead to the future."

Dad was all about living in the moment, so I wasn't surprised by his answer. I wished it had been different, though. I couldn't fully relax until this trip no longer felt like a test, but he was right that I wouldn't have nearly as much fun if I kept thinking about volleyball instead of appreciating the challenge right in front of me.

We kept at it for hours. Molly ran mostly in our tracks—wandering a bit now and then to investigate but never going beyond where she could catch a whiff of any changes to my blood sugar and give me a heads-up when necessary. We stayed on the ridgeline as much as possible, or on the side of the slope the wind hit. Not only was the traveling easier that way, but it was safer, too. Valleys and slopes, where the snow was deeper and protected from wind, had an increased risk of avalanches.

I don't know who was more worn out when we finally arrived at Summit Hut—my dog or me. Dad powered through, finding a shovel first thing. He cleared the front stoop while I explored inside.

I hadn't known what to expect from the hut, but I loved what I found. The entire downstairs was one open room with a kitchen and eating area centered around a wood-burning stove. Large windows with sweeping views of the divide lined an entire side of the hut, and the most inviting padded window seats sat below them. As soon as I removed her saddlebag, Molly ran and leaped up on one of the seats. She wagged her tail while taking in the sights of the frigid world outside. The one we'd just stepped in from.

"I know what you mean," I said. "This is turning out to be some adventure, isn't it, girl?" Once we'd gotten past a few glitches, the rest of the day had been spectacular. And now . . . don't get me wrong—I'd loved every second we spent outdoors—but it felt even better to be indoors. Here we could observe the beauty of the massive snowcapped peaks from a place of warmth and comfort.

All the doubts I'd had about coming on this trip had evaporated now that we'd made it to our first stop. One day at a time, one hut at a time—I'd manage my glucose levels, challenge myself, and have a ton of fun.

"Come on," I told Molly, "I'll race you upstairs!"

She stayed right on my heels as I climbed the flight of steps to the second level. I threw doors open, one after the other. Each room had several simple beds. I picked one of the smaller rooms for Dad, Molly, and me, and laid my pack down on the floor. It felt amazing to finally have the weight off.

I dug out my cell phone. Unsurprisingly, I didn't have

service. At some point we must have passed through an area that did, though, because I had two new text messages.

The first one was from Mom: **Hope you're having a good time and staying safe!**

The second one was Tanner: **Want to hang out today?**

Even though I knew it would fail, I typed a response to Tanner anyway—**Can't. Sorry**—and then watched the red exclamation mark pop up next to it on my screen.

I'd told him about the trip ages ago, right after Dad and I planned it, but I hadn't reminded him recently because I knew he'd think it was a bad idea. Now it was clear he'd either forgotten about it or assumed we'd canceled. I got a familiar sinking feeling in my stomach. Our friendship was so much more complicated now.

We were shooting hoops one day, not long after my diagnosis, and out of the blue he said, "It's scary, you know."

"What is? My three-point shot? Yeah, it can be a little intimidating," I'd joked, and passed him the ball.

He hadn't cracked even a hint of a smile. Worse, he just stood there holding the ball, all serious-like. "Not knowing," he said. His honey-brown eyes pierced through me. "Look, I want to be there for you. But I can't because you won't tell me anything anymore."

Honestly, I hadn't really thought about what it was like

for him. Our parents talked. He knew when I was in the hospital. He'd sent me text messages and gone with me the first time I'd met Molly. But he was right, I'd never opened up to him about what it had been like. I didn't tell him about what happens to me when my levels go out of range, or even that I was learning how to control it.

"You made things easier for me when I had a broken arm. I want to help you like you helped me."

When we were in fourth grade, Tanner fell riding a skateboard and broke his left wrist. He's left-handed, so I let him borrow my notes. I carried his books. I even helped him zip up his jacket for recess. But it was temporary. After a month he got his cast off and everything went back to normal. Things would never go back to normal for me. It was okay if I needed extra attention from the school nurse and my parents and coaches and teachers, but not Tanner.

"You can't," I said. "I'm fine. Just . . . just shoot the ball already."

I didn't want to always feel like I was dragging him down, and I didn't want him going easy on me. I just wanted to feel like we were on an even playing field. Not only when we were playing sports, either. All the time.

Sure, he was going to be upset that I'd left town without telling him, but there was nothing I could do about it at this point. Plus, I'd rather have him mad at me than worrying the entire time I was gone. I shoved my phone back in my pack then, and because I knew it was time and Dad was busy readying the hut for our stay, I checked my levels without him having to remind me.

"All good," I told Molly, and I swear the look she gave me was practically a smile.

"Emily." Dad's voice rang up the stairs. "Can you give me a hand?"

I liked that he hadn't asked if I was okay. Instead of telling me to rest or take another test, he wanted my help. "Be right there!" I said, feeling better than ever.

CHAPTER 9

By the time Molly and I returned downstairs, Dad had the wood-burning stove lit, and the hut felt even cozier. He grinned at me and seemed as pleased with our first day as I was. I thought he might even be a little impressed that I was still going strong. Yes! That was my goal, after all.

"We need to melt some snow for drinking water," he said, and handed me an empty bucket.

We scooped snow outside and carried it in to boil on the stove. Then we hung our socks on a drying rack before really settling in. There were books and board games and even some toys in an alcove. Dad and I were on our second game of Yahtzee when the front door swung open and three skiers blew in along with a blast of frigid air. The huts worked on a system where anyone wanting to explore the backcountry could reserve a bed for the night. That way the huts could provide more lodging for a higher number of travelers, instead of being occupied by private parties all the time.

I used to like meeting new people, and I never minded when they'd say something along the lines of "Tell me about yourself!" Since my diagnosis, though, strangers and their questions made me feel apprehensive. Dad stood up at the same time I hunkered lower in my seat. Meanwhile, the skiers began shedding layers and hanging gear on the hooks in the entryway. I'm not the best at guessing ages, but I'd say the two guys and the girl were in their early twenties. Their faces were ruddy from the change in temperature.

"Mmm, it's so toasty in here," the young woman said, rubbing her newly unmittened hands together.

"Right?" the taller of the two guys chimed in. "Note to self, always arrive after another group."

"I'm Mike," Dad said, and thrust out his hand.

The second guy, who wasn't much taller than me and whose black hair was sticking out in all directions, shook Dad's hand. "Ahmad. Nice to meet you."

"This is Emily"—Dad gestured toward me—"and that's Molly."

I gestured to Molly, so she knew it was okay to leave my side and go greet the newcomers. While the other two introduced themselves as Dan and Chloe, she ran circles around the group, familiarizing herself with their scents and begging to be petted. I'd yet to meet anyone who didn't cave to her charms. She collected a back scratch from each of them before dutifully returning to my side.

"I didn't know dogs were allowed," Chloe said.

I shifted uncomfortably. We'd gotten special permission to bring Molly. "She's a service dog," I said, and left it at that. I didn't want the woman to bombard me with questions if I revealed why I needed Molly's assistance.

Chloe gazed at me intently. She was pretty—glowing skin, shiny auburn hair, and large blue-green eyes. I knew she was trying to figure out what type of service I could possibly need. I did my best not to wither under her scrutiny.

"Come on, let's put our bags upstairs," Dan said, breaking the awkwardness of the moment.

When the three left the room, I let out a large breath of air.

Dad smiled lopsidedly. "I'm sure she didn't mean anything by it."

I nodded and smiled faintly back at him. He was right. No doubt, Chloe was only curious, and I could have told her why we'd brought Molly along—that the dog helped keep me safe. I just didn't want to feel like my diabetes had to be the first thing anyone knew about me.

By the time the three returned, the conversation had, thank goodness, moved on. While I cleaned up the board games Dad and I had dragged out, he fell into an easy discussion with the strangers about their route and how long they'd been out for. Unlike Dad and me, they were on the tail end of their adventure.

"FYI," Dan said, "we saw some very large canine tracks in the snow earlier today."

"Large canine?" Dad said. "Coyote? Dog?"

"I don't think so," Dan said. "Paws were too big. Sharp claws. Pretty sure they were wolf tracks. Pack of three or four would be my guess."

I shivered at the same time Dad humphed. "Not likely," he said. "Wolves were eradicated from Colorado decades ago."

Dan shrugged. "Whatever, man. Just telling you what we saw. And as far as I know, wolves don't care a darn about state lines. With reintroduction happening all over the Midwest, they're bound to wind up here."

Dad cast me a fleeting glance. I could tell he didn't want to believe Dan but had his concerns. "Well, the only canine we have to worry about for now is Molly. She might go feral if we don't feed her soon."

"As will I," Ahmad said, rubbing his stomach.

While the adults worked on dinner, I poured a cup of dog food in a bowl for Molly, then got out my kit. And that's all it took for me to feel like I was back under a microscope with Chloe. She had the satisfied look of someone who'd put together all the pieces. I tried to ignore her while I finished testing, and instead focused my attention on Dad as we calculated the carbs in the food I was about to eat, and then figured out how much bolus insulin I should take.

It felt weird to have people watching, so after Dad gave me the injection in a different room, the five of us sat at the long kitchen table. Because the other travelers had extra food and were nearing the end of their trip, Dad had accepted when they offered to share their meal. The pad thai was just how I liked it—salty and nutty with a hint of sweet.

I was glad Dad took them up on their offer. That is, until Ahmad offered me a slice of banana bread after dinner.

"Oh, you probably shouldn't have any," Chloe said as I reached toward the plate. "It has a ton of sugar."

I yanked my hand back, blushing with a mixture of anger and embarrassment. I was so tired of hearing "advice" from people who had no idea what they were talking about. The worst was when people made it sound like if I'd only eaten healthier, I never would've gotten diabetes in the first place. In fact, there were a number of things that could have caused it, but my diet wasn't one of them. It had been a long day, though, and I wasn't up to combating misconceptions. So I said no thanks to the bread and excused myself from the table.

I went straight to check out the books on the shelves, hoping to find something I could lose myself in and ignore the strangers for the rest of the evening. Unfortunately, there were books for small children and books for adults, but not much in between. I settled on a nonfiction book about the Tenth Mountain Division, mostly because I'd seen the name on some of the hut reservation paperwork, but I wasn't sure what it was.

It didn't take me long to find out. The first paragraph read:

> The Tenth Mountain Division of the U.S. Army was an elite group of alpine soldiers who pushed back the Nazis on the dividing line between Germany and Italy in February of 1945, thereby turning the tide of World War II. Winter was itself a formidable enemy, and the critical cold weather survival techniques learned while training at Camp Hale in Leadville, Colorado, gave these brave soldiers the upper hand in some of the harshest terrain on the planet. The best skiers in the world were recruited to join the Tenth Mountain Division and it was some of these men who made the modern ski industry what it is today.

I'd been skiing for almost my entire life, and I'd never given much thought to how it became a popular sport. As I read on, I learned how veterans from the Tenth Mountain

Division returned to Colorado and created multiple ski areas and how the technology that was developed for the ski soldiers made skiing more accessible for people who otherwise couldn't afford to give it a try. Also, I thought it was really cool that some of the huts we'd be staying at were built in honor of the Tenth Mountain Division, using funds donated by veterans.

It wasn't the type of book I'd normally read, but I liked that it had a connection to where we were staying. Not to mention that it appeared to be my best option. I took it with me upstairs and settled into my sleeping bag for the night. Molly climbed up beside me on the bed. I kept turning the pages, looking at photos and skimming the text. Letters from an eighteen-year-old army soldier caught my attention and I read the first one:

March 8th, 1943

Dear Folks,

I've up and joined an intriguing new unit in the Army. It's for skiers and mountaineers, you know, the adventurous sort. Don't worry about me. With my background and training,

I'll be right at home. I'm catching a train to Fort Devens for induction first thing in the morning. Traveling first class Pullman on the government's dime. Can you believe it? Well, I'm pooped and better get some rest. I'll write more when I get shipped.

Love,

Will

At first, I didn't know why his entry was so interesting to me. I'd never been drawn to books on war before. Then it hit me that battles, large and small, had been on my mind a lot lately. Sometimes, Coach Vega said we "battled our way to victory" when we won a difficult match. Dr. Morlock had described what I was going through as a "battle" against diabetes. I'd overheard a conversation Mom had with a friend about "picking your battles." She'd been talking about the decision to let me go on this trip. Apparently, I'd won that battle. Or had it been waged between her and Dad behind closed doors? Then there were all the battles between my parents that they hadn't hidden from me—countless arguments over money or Dad missing a commitment that had been important to Mom.

I knew that none of our problems came anywhere close to the scale of World War II, where millions of lives had been at stake. But I did wonder what compelled Will to join such a massive battle. I knew from history class that sometimes soldiers had no choice and were drafted into war. But that hadn't been the case with Will. He'd been eighteen, only five years older than me, when he decided to put his life on the line and fight for something bigger than himself.

I found his bravery inspiring. I wanted to know more about what happened to him, but by then, Molly was lightly snoring, and I could barely keep my eyes open. I fell asleep with the book on my chest, feeling worn out and satisfied with the first day of my own adventure. And I felt excited about what lay ahead. I knew there would be unpleasant things about this trip—like Chloe's rudeness and having to remove my gloves in the cold to get a reading—but it felt like more happy moments than not were in my future, and that wasn't something I'd been able to say for a long time.

CHAPTER 10

Waking up in a bed that wasn't my own was confusing. For a fuzzy moment, I forgot where I was. Then I saw how frost gave the windows lacy corners, and it all came back to me. It was plenty warm inside the hut thanks to the wood-burning stove, but outside was another story.

I hadn't heard Dad come into our room during the night, but I could tell, by the lumps in his sleeping bag, he was still asleep. So was Molly. At two, she wasn't that far past the puppy stage, but she'd been tuckered out by all the snow and activity the day before. I ran my fingers through her fur, and she let out a groggy but happy groan in reply. Molly was the best. I couldn't have asked for a better service dog, but I remembered Mom's warning that Molly couldn't detect my levels 100 percent of the time. "Would you have even noticed if I'd gone hypo through the night?" I whispered in her ear. She groaned a second time.

Not wanting to disturb Dad, I opted to stay in bed a bit longer. The book I'd started the night before had fallen to the floor. I retrieved it and read the next entry. I had to know what happened to Will. Did he regret his decision? Was he forced to sacrifice too much?

March 21st, 1943

Dear Mom and Pop,

It's been a thrilling few weeks. I've hardly had a chance to sit down. I'm now writing from training at Camp Hale, Colorado. I feel great and the other mountain troopers in my barracks are just swell. We are fully equipped with rucksacks and skis and we're quickly learning the ropes. Our CO (commanding officer) keeps us going at a terrific pace with sixty to ninety pounds of gear on our backs. It's a good thing I was fit as a fiddle coming in, or I'd never make it up the mountain. As for the skiing, what a gas! There's plenty of snow, but it's melting fast. We'll be moving to the higher slopes to train soon.

Yours,

Will

P.S. Please send cookies.

What Will was going through sounded difficult, but so far, he didn't seem to mind. In fact, some of the training sounded fun, but it was just training, not actual battle. I lost myself in the entries until Molly stirred beside me and began pawing my leg. The book had occupied my attention and I'd failed to notice that my mouth had gone dry, and beads of sweat were forming on the back of my neck. When I sat up in bed, I felt a little dizzy. Molly had detected what I hadn't. It was clear my blood sugar levels had dropped while I was reading.

"Okay, you redeemed yourself," I said to Molly, and snagged my kit from the dresser beside my bed. Sure enough, my levels were low. If my levels stayed low for too long, my body would stop functioning properly. I could lose consciousness, have a seizure, or worse. I popped four glucose tabs in my mouth and let them dissolve on my tongue. Then I flipped the book back open while I waited to retest.

In the next few letters, Will went into more detail describing how hard it was to scale the mountains with all that gear, but how the payoff of downhill skiing made it all worth it. He loved some of the same things I loved about the backcountry: the trees, being able to see for miles in all directions when you reached the top of a slope, the thrill of speeding down the mountain on two sticks and controlling the way they sliced through the snow.

Fifteen minutes flew by. When I tested, I wasn't sweating, and my head no longer felt like I'd just stepped off a Tilt-A-Whirl. I was back in a normal range, but I also knew I needed breakfast soon or I'd go low again.

I crept over to Dad's bed and nudged him awake. Even though I'd been gentle, he shot up in bed anyway. "Oh!" he said. "I guess I was more wiped out than I thought. I overslept."

When we made it downstairs, there was a short note jotted on the whiteboard by the door:

Great meeting you both, but adventure calls!

Safe travels, Ahmad, Chloe, and Dan

I can't say I was disappointed that they'd already left and that Dad and I had the hut all to ourselves again. I was due for another injection, and the trip was far more enjoyable when I didn't feel like a specimen under a microscope.

After I calculated how much I needed and Dad gave me a bolus of insulin with the pen, Dad whipped up some pancakes with dried coconut flakes sprinkled on top. He liked to brag about being an Eagle Scout and earning his cooking merit badge when he was a little older than I was now. But the reality of it was, he rarely cooked anything other than instant noodles at home. Maybe cooking was a little like riding a bike, though, because the pancakes were delicious.

When he took a bite, his eyes practically rolled backward in his head. "I don't know why, but food just tastes better in the mountains."

I had to agree. Even though we'd forgone maple syrup because it was messy and too heavy (we'd gone for lightweight and calorie-dense food items), the pancakes were just the right amount of chewy and sweet.

After breakfast, we took our time cleaning the hut and repacking our gear. The thermostat mounted to the window frame said it was only 3 degrees outside. Dad said we could "wait for the sun to warm things up a bit before *we* answered the call of adventure."

Anxious to find out more about Will and the other "ski troopers" before I had to leave the book behind, I pulled the paperback out once more and curled up in one of the big, cozy window seats. A thought hit me as I was settling in. "We're coming back to this hut on our last night, right?" I asked Dad. We were going the same route as Chloe and her group, and they said they'd circled back to here.

"Yes, we are," he said. "Why?"

"Do you think I can borrow this book?" I hadn't gotten to the part where Will left for the war yet. He was brave, but it must've turned everything upside down for him and I wanted to see how he'd been affected.

"I don't see why not. It won't add much weight to your load," he said. Then after a pause, he added, "An athlete and a scholar. I couldn't be prouder."

I smiled softly back at him. He meant it as a compliment, but I wasn't so sure I could live up to his expectations on either front, at least not these days.

It did warm up outside, but not by much. The sky was grayer than the day before, and flurries swirled in the air around us. The peaks were intimidatingly tall, and it bothered me some that I couldn't see our tracks coming in from the day before. I could only guess at the direction we'd come.

Almost as soon as we set out, I was looking forward to getting to the next hut and warming my hands with a mug of hot chocolate. But that was before we hit the downhill section of our trail. Nothing, not even the promise of a sweet hot drink, could've dragged me indoors then.

I was super thankful to have the extra grippy-ness of the skins when I needed them, but even more thankful when I got to take them off. After the previous day of all uphill and flats, it felt amazing to tuck and lean into the pull of gravity. I nearly squealed as I picked up speed and shot past Dad, carving out a winding path through the powder. Molly barreled along beside me, her tongue hanging out and her tail wagging with delight.

I thought of Will. It was clear from his letters that he enjoyed much of his training, even though the conditions were harsh. But it was one thing to be challenged by instruction and drills, and something else to truly have your mettle tested. So far, I'd only read about the difficulties Will faced at Camp Hale. In his letters he still sounded determined and resolute. Would that change when he went to war?

I could sort of understand some of what he was going through as he prepared for battle. Skiing was exhilarating, but it was hard work, too, and often painful. That was true for many sports. During volleyball season, my muscles ached regularly, and the skin on my forearms stung whenever I bumped the ball. That didn't stop me from loving every minute of it. There was nothing like working together with my teammates, and the rush of victory when we won a match.

Still, despite the discomfort—the breathlessness, the bruised knees, and floor-burned elbows—spirit on the court was easy compared to battles with bigger consequences. Ones like the balancing act I faced while managing my diabetes in the wilderness. If I was being honest, I was doubting myself more than I cared to admit. I wished I could borrow some of Will's bravery.

The bottom of the hill came all too soon. I turned my skis parallel and skidded to a stop.

"Nicely done," Dad said, rotating his skis to match mine and sending a spray of snow in my and Molly's direction. Even if I was doubting myself, I seemed to be doing an okay job of impressing Dad. At least, at the moment. I knew he didn't want to talk about sponsoring the Impalers yet, but the more compliments I earned, the more likely it seemed.

I beamed back at him while Molly shook the snow from her coat and stared up at us expectantly. "Now what?" I asked.

"Now you lead," he said. My stomach fell. I wasn't so sure I wanted to, not after I'd nearly gotten us lost shortly after we started our journey. I didn't want to disappoint Dad, though. I had to keep the praise coming and prove I wasn't a drag to be around. *I'm brave and confident*, I told myself. *I can face any battle.* Then I inwardly rolled my eyes at myself. I needed to impress my dad, not sound like him.

"Sure," I said. Instead of handing me his phone to follow the GPS app, he pulled out one of the topographical maps he'd printed off his computer.

I pinched it between my gloved fingers and stared at it, trying to make sense of what I was seeing. The curvy lines were called contour lines and they connected areas of the same elevations. So I knew that the tighter circles were peaks and that the closer the lines were to one another, the steeper the land. Lines that were farther apart meant the slope was more gradual. I located the marker with the name Summit Hut beside it and knew it was where we'd stayed the night before. Dad said we were headed to a smaller hut called Creek Pass. It took me a moment, but I found it as well. From there, I found an unlined area between them, and guessed that it was the valley we were standing in now.

I took a chance and pointed to a spot. "Are we here?"

"Just about," Dad said. "See the blue line? That's the stream that runs through the valley. We're not quite there yet. Probably another half mile or so, then we'll follow it to the next hut."

"Okay," I said. At least I'd come close to pinpointing our location. "I think I can handle that."

I shuffled my right ski forward. Dad said, "Aren't you forgetting something?" and tapped his thumb and middle finger together.

I couldn't believe two hours had passed since we left the hut. At school, I had a set schedule and the times I needed to use my kit were built into the day. Even on the weekends, I had a regular routine. Granted, there were unplanned checks when I felt off, or when Molly pawed at my leg. But it was so easy to lose track of time and forget in the back-country, where everything moved at a slower, dreamlike pace—even when, or maybe *especially* when, I was whipping down a mountain on skis.

The chill of the air hit me the second I removed my left glove. The first few weeks of testing, I switched fingertips every time I tested. Still, the skin on each turned purplish blue. I didn't bruise as easily now, and I found my index finger was the least sensitive. I don't know if it was numb from the cold or I was just used to it by now, but I hardly felt anything. After the prick, a ruby-red bead of blood formed on the tip of my finger. The shock of color seemed so out of place in the frosty world around us. I awkwardly maneuvered the strip with my gloved right hand to absorb the droplet. My glucose meter displayed the number right away, and I smiled. "We're good to go!"

The entire process took only a few minutes this time, and I was thrilled that we didn't have to wait for me to retest. I felt great as I steadily forged a path to the creek. Once we reached it, however, I couldn't help but hit the pause button. The same way a red drop of blood had seemed out of place surrounded by pure white snow, the movement of a river seemed out of place surrounded by the stillness of winter.

While I waited for Dad to catch up, I watched the water flowing around the snow and cascading over rocks. I listened to the gurgle it made where it bubbled near the edges beneath thin sheets of ice. Of all the landscapes I'd seen so far on this trip, this was my favorite.

"I don't believe it," Dad said.

At first, I thought he was talking about the breathtaking beauty of the river, but when I turned toward his voice, I found him crouched down, peering at something in the snow. I glided over to see what it was: paw prints, similar to Molly's, but far larger.

"Wolf?" I asked.

Dad nodded. "That kid was right." I knew he meant Dan. Apparently, my dad was now of the age where he considered anyone under thirty a "kid."

The back of my neck tingled as a chill ran up my spine. I couldn't help but nervously glance about. "Are we in danger?"

"No," Dad said decisively. "Wolves are cautious animals and typically aren't interested in humans. Attacks are exceedingly rare."

I wanted to believe him, but he'd been wrong about the tracks. Could he be wrong about the risk the wolves posed to us as well?

"Just to be safe, let's leash Molly for the rest of the day."

I signaled for Molly to come, and she immediately ran to my side. She'd been trained to be under strict voice command, but I wasn't sure how she'd respond if she encountered a wolf pack. Her leash was in her saddlebag. I fished it out and clipped it to her collar. "Good girl," I said.

It wasn't long before my energy took a nosedive. But I knew we were getting close to the next hut, and I didn't want to lose the ground I felt I'd made by impressing Dad with my downhill skiing and my navigational skills. I reasoned that I was a normal amount of tired considering the day I'd had. Plus, it hadn't been two hours yet since I'd last tested, had it?

Each tree looked like the last. The breeze picked up. Even though it wasn't snowing, snowflakes were being blown from the tree branches and swirling in the air. I focused my attention on finding trail blazes and propelling myself forward. Maybe it was because there was so much white everywhere I looked, but I didn't notice when my vision turned blurry. I didn't notice what terrible shape I was in until I found myself slumped over in the snow with Dad beside me, my head cradled in his lap.

There was a straw inside my mouth and cool liquid sliding down my throat. *How had it gotten there? Oh, right. Dad.*

"Emily, Emily, Emily!" He repeated my name until my eyes trained on his. I saw right through him, into the depths of his fear. "Keep sipping. Don't you fall asleep."

I sucked more sweetness from the juice box. My skin tingled, my head spun, and my heart thudded. I felt weepy and scared. This was bigger than an annoying interruption. This was serious. If I lost consciousness now, there was a good chance I wouldn't wake up. Ever.

It was comforting to have Dad there, and to know he was intent on not letting that happen. Once I finished the fruit punch, he gave me a small handful of glucose tablets.

Still, it was a good fifteen to twenty minutes before my head cleared and I stopped feeling shaky. I smiled back at him sheepishly. "I'm okay," I said. Dad heaved a sigh of relief, and Molly crowded in and nuzzled my head with hers. She seemed to be apologizing.

"It's all right, girl. It wasn't your fault." Between the breeze, the distance that had been between us, and a wolf scent likely still lingering in the air, I couldn't blame her for missing my dropping blood sugar. I could, however, blame myself. I should've been paying closer attention to what my body had been trying to tell me.

The fear in Dad's eyes quickly morphed into something else when he saw I was going to be all right. "Maybe your mom was right," he grumbled under his breath. He glanced back the direction we'd come, and I worried he was thinking about calling it quits.

I sat up too quickly and my brain whirled inside my head. I flicked my eyes shut and then opened them again when I felt a bit steadier. "It won't happen again," I said.

"You don't know that."

He was right. I didn't. A moment of absolute silence followed while I held my breath and hoped he wouldn't say it was time to turn around.

When he did speak, he said, "It's going to be dark soon. Let's just make sure you're okay and then get to the next hut." His words and demeanor revealed nothing about his plans for the trip beyond our next stop.

I let out the breath I'd been holding, but I couldn't let go of all my apprehension as I drew out my kit. Any ground I'd made with my dad had been totally wiped out. I wanted to think this was just a little glitch, and that I could prevent it next time. The truth was, though, I was at the mercy of my illness and the winter elements. I had very little, if any, control, and that was as frustrating as it was frightening.

CHAPTER 11

It was twilight when we reached the hut. The combination of my goggle lenses and the setting sun cast an orange glow to the tallest peaks. It had been a near-perfect day. That was, up until the point I'd collapsed in the snow. Ever since, it'd felt like a low-lying cloud had drifted between Dad and me.

At least we'd have this hut all to ourselves. It was much smaller than the first—a single room with a set of bunk beds instead of multiple rooms and levels. It had an even cozier feel because of it, but that also meant there was no place for me to go to escape Dad's unrest.

He brooded while we stripped off our wet layers and he got the wood-burning stove lit. Like the first hut, there was no electricity. There were solar-powered light bulbs, but that was it. Before long, however, the fire in the stove had warmed the hut, we were melting snow for drinking water, and Dad had supper simmering in a pan. Molly was curled up at the base of the stove. I finally felt relaxed enough to wrap myself in a blanket and settle in on the couch.

I was about to crack open my book on the Tenth Mountain

Division when my phone dinged. Dad stopped stirring the pot. "What do you know? We must have service here."

I pulled it out and looked at the screen. Mom again: **Gosh the house is quiet without you and Molly here. Love and miss you bunches!**

A tiny knot formed in the pit of my stomach. I missed Mom, too. If she knew I had service, she'd want to chat. A year ago, I would've been dying to call her. But now . . . with Dad teetering, I didn't want a phone call with Mom to send him over the edge. I knew she'd drill me with a million questions about how I was feeling, and if I was being careful.

"Was it your mom?" Dad asked. "You should probably give her a call while you can. There's a good chance we won't have service for the rest of the trip, and she's probably worried sick about you."

I froze. *The rest of the trip?* Did that mean we weren't turning around? Maybe his angst had thawed with the warming of the hut. I certainly didn't want to do anything to bring back his doubts. I was stuck. Just the thought of calling Mom filled me with trepidation, but revealing that to Dad might set off red flags. I had to call her.

She picked up on the first ring. "Emily!" Her voice was full of sunshine and warmth. I could tell she was smiling the way she does when her entire face lights up.

My face lit up, too, despite the twinge of guilt I felt for even thinking about not calling her. "I miss you, too, Mom," I said. And, of course, I spent the next five minutes reassuring her that I was monitoring my levels, that I was perfectly safe, and that the trip was going great. Dad was listening to my side of the conversation. Thankfully, he kept his mouth shut and didn't make me fess up about the scare we'd had that afternoon.

Mom sounded even more nervous when she moved on from my health concerns to tell me that the news was reporting a winter storm heading toward the high country.

"Please let your dad know," she said, and then waited.

"Now?" I asked.

"Now."

Darn. It didn't seem like a great time to be springing anything else on him that might sway him in the wrong direction. Still, I dutifully lowered the phone beneath my chin and relayed the info.

"Uh-huh," he responded absently. It seemed he was preoccupied with not burning our meal. Maybe it wouldn't be as big a deal as I thought. "Did they say where?"

"Did they say where?" I asked Mom.

"Oh, you know how the news is. Lots of swirly marks all over the weather map, not a lot of detail."

"Nope," I told Dad. "You know how *unreliable* weather reports are," I added, hoping if I didn't take it seriously, he wouldn't, either.

He nodded. "I'm sure it's nothing, but since we have service, I'll look into it after dinner."

Phew, I thought, *maybe we're out of the woods*. Then I inwardly laughed at myself. That was the worst expression that could've crossed my mind. It was the opposite of what I wanted. I wanted my parents to let me *stay* in the woods. At least for a few more days.

"One other thing . . ." Mom's voice rang in my ear.

"Yeah?" I snapped back to attention.

"Tanner stopped by the house yesterday."

"Oh." Another reason to dread going back to the real world. I'd have to face Tanner. Me ghosting him by going on this trip without letting him know I was leaving would only make things more awkward between us.

"He seemed upset when I told him you'd be gone until the end of the week."

The twinge of guilt I'd felt before grew into a surge. It really hadn't been fair for me to leave without saying goodbye. "Okay," I said.

"Are you going to call him?"

I shrugged even though she couldn't see it. "I don't

know," I said. I knew I should, but I didn't need to seek out more complicated conversations when things with Dad were already touch and go.

There was a long pause on the other end. Then Mom said, "I'm not going to tell you how to run your relationships . . ."

Translation: She was about to tell me exactly how to run my relationships. "But, to have a friend, you have to be a friend, and that means you have to follow the golden rule and—"

I interrupted her before she rattled off another tired expression. "I should go, Mom, my battery's getting low."

"Okay, honey, I love you! Don't forget to—"

I was pretty sure she was going to say "keep checking your levels" or "stay on top of your carbs," or something along those lines. Instead, she said, "Say hi to your dad and give Molly a hug for me."

"Yeah, okay, see ya," I said, and hung up. I guess it was nice that she acknowledged Dad, but what did it say about *their* relationship that Molly was the one she was sending a hug to?

I opened my contact list and scrolled down until I found Tanner's name. My thumb lingered there for a second while I debated giving him a call. If I was being honest with myself, things had gotten strange between us even before I got sick. It used to be so easy to talk about anything and everything.

Most of it was silly stuff, like how we both hated artichoke dip and preferred juice boxes over fruit drink pouches because of straw issues.

Middle school had changed everything. It was like every little thing got supercharged with meaning—who you hung out with, how you dressed, how you looked at a person, what got posted on social media. I was more cautious about the things I said and did, not wanting my words or actions to be taken the wrong way. I could tell Tanner was, too. And that made it even harder to know what to say to him at a time like this, when I knew I hadn't been a good friend. I didn't know how to make it okay between us. But I did know that we could never go back to the way things were before. So I closed my contacts, hooked my phone up to Dad's portable battery charger, and took out my book.

It crossed my mind that when it came to dealing with Tanner and Dad, I could use a shot of courage. I really envied Will's bravery.

April 7th, 1943

Dear Mom and Pop,

We took a long hike yesterday. My boots are tough, and my socks are thick, but you wouldn't believe the blisters on my feet. I'm on the basketball team, too. Did I tell you that? Between practices, sharpshooting, guard duty, and studying my orders, I don't know whether I'm coming or going half the time. We have an unofficial motto, Sempre Avanti. It's Italian for "Always Forward." Doesn't matter what we're doing, or what's in our way, we keep moving. It's great and all but gee whiz, I'm beat.

Love,

Will

P.S. The fellas really enjoyed the cookies!

I liked that Will and I had more in common than our love of skiing. He was an athlete, too. I wondered if I could adopt the motto of the Tenth Mountain Division. Sempre Avanti. "Always Forward." But I'd tried that today, right before I found myself slumped in the snow. Still, part of having courage was not accepting defeat. It meant getting back up after you'd fallen and carrying on. I'd done that, hadn't I? Yet, I was too chicken to give Tanner a call, so obviously I had plenty to learn. I kept reading.

May 16th, 1943

Dear Gram,

Mom said I had you to thank for the cookies.
Wow! They were delicious. I would've written
sooner, but we had another trip up and over
the mountains. It's called a bivouac and we
leave our tents and shelter behind. The days
were hard, and I spent the nights under the
stars with my sleeping bag rolled out over
my skis. I'm learning so much about winter
survival. Who knew pine needles had so many
uses? I've woven them with branches to fashion
snowshoes. I've shoved them in my coat and
pants for an extra layer of warmth, and I've
even used them to make tea. After this I
imagine I'll be ready for anything.

I'm getting a weekend pass to go fishing
with some of the guys. I'll be happy to have
a break from the army routine, but I'll be
ready when it's time to get back to training.

Love,

Will

After dinner, Dad checked the avalanche reports. I held my breath while he stared at his phone. His lips thinned, and shadows settled in the creases of his skin. He looked older and warier than I'd ever seen him. "I'm sorry, kiddo," he said. "I think we better shorten our trip. We'll return to Summit Hut tomorrow night instead of carrying on to Pine Valley. That will get us back in two days instead of four."

There was a loud thrumming in my ears as my heart beat its protest. Even though I'd feared this was coming, I couldn't believe it was happening. Mom was up-front with her concerns, but I'd forgotten how Dad quietly calculated and stewed and then, wham! came the bad news. And once he made a decision, he rarely budged.

But I couldn't go home now. Going home meant being back under Mom's nervous watch. It also meant facing Tanner. Worst of all, though, the trip would end on a sour note with Dad, and that meant failure at everything I'd set out to accomplish. Dad wouldn't remember my successes; he'd remember being scared that I'd have another incident with low blood sugar. That fear would lead to more doubt surrounding my abilities to play in a competitive league.

We'd had moments of pure joy and fun on this trip, but the final takeaway would be that I was weak and fragile—not someone he could face stormy weather with. It might've been a bit extreme, but my deepest darkest fear was that he'd think I wasn't worthy of his time. Maybe that wasn't quite true now, but if we cut the trip short, he wouldn't spend the extra days at home with me. He'd go right back to work. He wouldn't sponsor my team, and I'd see less and less of him until someday I might not see him at all.

A loud "NO!" burst from my lips.

"Excuse me?" Dad said.

"No," I said, quieter but just as firmly. "We can't quit now." Maybe I had learned something from Will. Yes, you had to pick your battles. But some things were so big, and so important, that fighting for them didn't feel like a choice. "We can't go home yet. You always say I should push myself to the max and test my limits. So, what changed?" I knew exactly what changed; I had diabetes now and he didn't think I was strong enough. "You've always been all about overcoming challenges and living life to the fullest. Then we found out I have diabetes, and it's like you no longer think those things apply to me. It's not fair."

Dad let out a wavering breath. "Don't do this, Em."

"Are the avalanche reports really that bad?" I pressed him. "Or are we going home because you're worried that I can't handle four more days in the wilderness?"

Dad shifted uncomfortably in his chair.

"That's it. Isn't it? You don't think I'm up for an extra challenge. Do you? Just tell me. If we'd done this trip last winter, before I ever got sick, would you still have made us go home?"

His Adam's apple bobbed. His silence said it all.

"I feel great," I argued. "We have plenty of supplies. The storm might not even come our direction. Are the avalanche reports really that bad?"

"Well, no," he admitted.

I looked him hard in the eye. "Please," I begged. "Don't give up on me."

He dropped his gaze first.

For a moment he did nothing. Then he was back to business. He picked up his phone and considered the map once more. "I suppose we could go a different route to the next hut . . . If we stayed along the ridge instead of the valley, the avalanche risk would be less, but we'd have to put in more miles. We'd need to leave early in the morning. It seems like the storm won't be coming in until late afternoon. I don't want to get stuck in it, but we'll be okay as long as we can make it to the next hut. The way back should be easier and even if we got snowed in for a day, we accounted for that in our packing. We have plenty of food and insulin. So . . ."

It was far from a heart-to-heart, but I had gotten through

to him. Hope ballooned in my chest. Maybe I was proving myself to him. Maybe this trip would strengthen our connection instead of dissolving it. "So . . . yes?" I hedged.

He breathed out heavily. "Yeah, okay. Seems like the biggest risk we're taking is that your mother might kill me if we make it back a day late."

I lunged across the kitchen table and gave him a hug, nearly knocking over our dinner dishes in the process. "Thanks, Dad!"

CHAPTER 12

February 21st, 1944

Dear Folks,

It's awfully cold. We've been living in tents for the past two weeks and at 30 below it's difficult to sit down and write. The skiing is swell, but I miss the summer months and rock climbing with bare hands. Now we wear two pairs of mittens over gloves. As I said, not the best conditions for writing. I can't believe it's been almost a year since I left home. How have I made it this long?

Love,

Will

We didn't wait for it to warm up again before setting out the following morning. It's a good thing we didn't because the sun never made an appearance. Heavy gray clouds made it difficult to distinguish where the snow ended and the sky began. It was the kind of cold that made my bones ache the moment I stepped outside. Skiing was a constant scraping through sharp ice crystals instead of gliding through powdery or billowy snow.

My hydration pack was entirely full of water we'd melted at the hut. I sipped on it slowly and munched on my trail food throughout the day. Dad said it wasn't uncommon for wolf territories to be as large as fifty square miles, so I kept Molly on her leash, not knowing which way the pack would roam.

It had snowed several inches while we slept, which was far from a major storm, but I could tell Dad was being extra careful in his route selection. The outdoor survival classes we took had taught us how to watch out for avalanche terrain. We stayed along the windblown side of the mountain again and avoided gullies and areas where there were downed trees or no trees. We watched for steep slopes and rocky cliffs loaded with snow. The cold temps and wind had caused a crusty layer to form on top of the new snow along the route we chose. I knew a dry layer of fresh powder on top of hardened snow would've been more dangerous, but it also would have been more enjoyable to ski across.

I don't know if it was Dad's mood that had me unsettled, or if it was the weather, but this day didn't have the same feel of thrill and excitement. The wind continued to pick up, and even though I didn't know the exact temperature, it was the coldest day of our trip by far. By midmorning, my fingers and toes felt numb. I was wearing liners under my mittens, and I fisted my hands to warm them. It didn't quite do the trick, so I broke out some hand warmer packets and shook them until heat radiated from the pouch.

Even so, when it came time to check my glucose levels, I had to rub my fingers and blow on them before I was able to squeeze out a single droplet of blood. We found a somewhat sheltered area in a grove of pines, but there wasn't any escaping the bitter cold.

"How are you holding up?" Dad asked.

Even though I'd been sipping plenty of water, my mouth felt dry. My heart beat a little too rapidly in my chest and my stomach hurt. I forced a smile and said I was "fine," but I was certain that if there wasn't so much wind and I wasn't wearing so many layers of clothing, Molly would be pawing at my leg in alarm. It took longer than usual with having to warm my fingers and all, but I finally got the readout and sure enough, my levels were too high.

Dad's eyes registered what I was thinking—pushing forward today instead of sheltering at Creek Pass or returning to Summit Hut had been a poor decision.

We calculated how much insulin I would need and removed one of the insulin pens from the cooler. Dad turned it the right number of clicks as I pulled up layer after layer to find my bare belly. The wind was blistering on my skin, and I shivered uncontrollably. I wasn't sure if it was from the cold or my glucose levels being off. The upside was, I was so numb by the time the needle pierced my skin that I hardly felt it.

The wind blew even harder, carrying snowflakes sideways with it. "It's really picking up," Dad said. He fumbled around to put his gloves back on. Then, between the layers and zippers, the wind and snow, he struggled to put the insulin storage pack in his backpack. Once it was secure, he pulled out his phone. While he studied our location on his GPS map, he shook his head and groaned. "At this point we're a tad closer to Pine Valley than Creek Pass. It doesn't make sense to turn around."

Putting on a brave face, I smiled at him through my balaclava—my teeth chattering the entire time. I could barely see his eyes through his goggles and his own face mask, but it's safe to say he wasn't smiling.

This time, instead of hanging out while we waited to recheck my levels, I stood up and bounced on my toes, trying to keep them warm. Dad didn't get up and he didn't say a thing. He didn't have to for me to tell what kind of mood he was in.

"Sorry," I said.

He looked up at me. "For what?"

"For this. For making us have to wait in a storm when we need to keep moving."

"Not your fault," he said, then fell silent again, like he knew how unconvincing he sounded.

After the fifteen minutes were up, I pulled out my kit to test again. Instead of slipping my meter back in my inside pocket, though, I'd left it with the kit. When I turned it on, it gave me an error message. "Uh . . ." I said, and showed it to Dad.

"It's this blasted cold." He took the meter from me, opened his winter coat, and placed it in the space between his arm and side. We waited a few more minutes in awkward silence as the wind bit through our layers and the snowfall steadily increased.

Luckily, when Dad withdrew it from inside his coat, it turned on right away. After a little more blowing on my fingers and rubbing them together, I was finally able to produce a drop of blood and we were back in business.

Dad let out a sigh of relief when he saw the readout. I thought he'd been in a bad mood because I'd delayed us yet again. But maybe it was more because he was nervous. We'd be in a real pickle if we couldn't get my numbers to go down. We were hours if not days away from getting to an ER if I needed one.

Once we were moving again, I thought about Will and his letters. The first ones had all been light and happy. He was obviously thrilled and excited to be training alongside his fellow snow soldiers. As time passed, though, his tone had grown more serious and uncertain. Some of his friends were starting to ship out, and some who were shipping out were never going to return home. So far, he hadn't said anything about wanting to quit, though, and he hadn't once mentioned regretting his decision to join the army. Instead, he said it didn't help to be anxious and there was nothing to do but "take things as they came."

Thinking about how he'd done his best to stay brave as he said goodbye to friends heading off to war, and his own departure date crept closer, helped me cling to a shred of courage.

I knew my situation was way different from his. Dad and I had chosen to come on this trip for recreation. Will had enlisted in the army to protect others. There were risks involved in both. I wasn't facing anything like an actual battlefield, but he was right that being anxious never helped. So I tried to stay calm as the storm intensified. Dad glanced back every few feet of progress to be sure Molly and I were still on his heels, or at least that he could still see us. Visibility was not so great, and it was getting worse.

Dad stopped right in front of me and pulled out his phone. "Dang," he said. "The cold got to my phone battery as well. It's completely dead." He hooked it up to his backup charger. "We've got to keep going. I saw a trail blaze recently. We should be fine." I think he was saying it as much for his benefit as for mine.

"We're only a few miles from the Pine Valley hut. Even in these conditions, we should be there in less than an hour," he added with deliberate calmness. However, he couldn't totally hide a slight quaver in his voice. Below the surface, I knew, he was fighting as hard as I was to keep fear in check.

I nodded. *Don't get anxious. It won't help.* It was a thought meant for us both. We were headed to a warm hut and a cozy spot by a wood-burning stove. It wasn't like I had to walk through gunfire to get there. I just had to make it through a little snow. But I couldn't help but think of the words at the beginning of the book. "Winter was itself a formidable enemy."

Just then, as if Winter was reading my mind and wished to prove how formidable it could be, it raised all its forces at once. The wind intensified. The snowflakes grew denser. They came more and more rapidly, until they blotted out everything in their path. In a matter of seconds, the world around us turned terrifyingly white.

CHAPTER 13

It felt like skiing through a dream. Everything around me was buffered. Sound, time, sight—all deadened by the winter storm. I kept my eyes trained on Dad's bright red ski jacket. The only color to be found in all the whiteness. It was a beacon, a life preserver. In that moment, it was the thing that mattered most.

I did everything I could to not lose the flash of crimson. *Less than an hour*, I repeated Dad's words to myself. This misery was temporary. It was escapable.

Or so I thought.

As quickly as I used my gloved hand to clear the flakes piling on my goggles, they were covered again. There was nothing but nature for miles and miles around, but I felt trapped, like I was suffocating from all that snow. My lungs contracted. A flash of Dad's jacket cut through the white. I lunged forward. I was desperate to clutch it with my fingertips and never let go. The swath of red was there, taunting me as I grasped for it. And then . . .

It was gone—swallowed whole by the blowing snow.

I halted in my tracks. I held very still. Everywhere I

looked, I saw nothing but colorless crystals. I lifted my gloved hand and waved it directly in front of my face. Nothing. It was as if the whiteout had caused me to go blind. "Dad!" I screamed into the void. Molly drew closer. Her body shook as she leaned against me, and we waited for a response.

Nothing. I forgot all about being brave. Absolute terror rose in my throat. Where was he? Then I heard a muffled cry. The blood coursing through my veins turned to ice.

"Daaaad!" I screamed again. But with the wind drowning out my voice and the world seemingly erased by snow, I felt utterly helpless. "Dad, where are you?"

I listened with all my might for any response. All I heard other than the wind whipping in my ears was the sound of Molly whimpering beside me. Even though her black fur was a stark contrast to the snow, I could barely make out her form.

I was petrified with fear and had no idea what to do. It wasn't my first time being caught in whiteout conditions. When it happened before, though, I'd been on a ski slope. It had been a little scary but mostly thrilling. I knew if I stayed away from the trees, I'd be okay. The powder was amazing, and I'd felt safe within the confines of the run for the few minutes it had lasted.

Here, though, it wasn't thrilling in the slightest. Not when there could be countless unseen dangers. But I couldn't just stay paralyzed. Something had happened to Dad. I needed to find out what.

The sound of my heartbeat pounded in my ears. I took deep, long breaths as I ran my mitten along Molly's backside, trying to calm us both. The fear made my head feel foggy. I focused my thoughts the best I could. The snow was blinding, but I could feel for obstacles and changes in the slope. I lifted my poles and used them to prod the snow in front of me. When I felt it was safe, I inched my way forward.

I carried on at a snail's pace, and Molly stayed right in step. I was thankful she'd been leashed as the storm swiftly moved in. If she hadn't, I'd have been separated from her as well.

I kept prodding the ground in front of me, alternating poles until I stuck the right one forward and felt nothing. I poked the air, searching for ground, and didn't find any. I stumbled backward on my skis as my breath caught in my throat. With the low visibility we must've veered off course. We'd wandered too close to the ridge. There was a drop-off right in front of me. Dad wasn't there. I didn't want to think about what that meant.

I couldn't believe this was happening. It didn't feel real, but I knew it wasn't a dream. Our trip had been great until everything had changed in an instant.

"Dad!" I screamed again. "Dad!"

No answer. Molly whimpered a second time, and then panic really set in. My body felt like it was caught in a cyclone of fear. I wanted to be brave, but all I could do was stand there and tremble. My teeth chattered and then I was the one whimpering. Molly moved closer. The pressure of her on my leg was soothing. It brought me back from the dark thoughts that had engulfed me as quickly as Dad had disappeared.

My head cleared slightly. There was nothing I could do for him while the wind was still whipping snow around and it was impossible to see. I didn't know how far Dad had fallen. It could be that the drop-off was short. He might have safely landed in a snowbank. I had to cling to that small hope. And I had to find shelter. It was too dangerous to continue searching for the hut, but I couldn't stay out in the open, either.

I turned away from the drop-off and began prodding the snow with my poles again. I didn't want to get too far away from where I'd last seen Dad, but I had to get out of the wind. The storm erased my tracks the second I made them. I could only pray that I'd be able to find this spot again once the blizzard died down.

I kept moving away from the ridgeline. Before the whiteout, we'd walked through a small cluster of trees. I thought I might be able to find it again, but the whiteout was so disorienting. If I wasn't on my feet, I wouldn't even know which way was up and which was down. I was shivering uncontrollably. Molly was bounding beside me, pawing at my leg in between lunges. I knew my glucose levels were dropping, but for once, that wasn't my first priority.

It felt like a miracle when my pole met something at about knee level. It wasn't air and wasn't soft, powdery snow. When I probed some more, I found there was nothing above waist level. So I reached out my mittened hands and investigated the object in front of me. I knew right away that it was a tree that had fallen over. Skiing beside it, I guided myself and Molly along until I found branches.

I clicked out of my skis, removed my backpack, and slid them both below the branches. Then I dropped to my knees and crawled forward while coaxing Molly to join me. The branches scraped my jacket, hat, and snow pants as I burrowed in as deep as I could go. I positioned myself on top of the skis, remembering how Will had slept on his. It was better than being on the snow, the chill of which I knew would seep through my clothing.

It was uncomfortable, but it was the best option I had. At least, tucked under the branches, the wind wasn't nearly as cutting.

Molly pressed against me, and I was thankful for her body heat. I dug into my bag and went straight for the survival kit. I busted out the thin emergency blanket and wrapped it around both of us. The shivering didn't stop. I retrieved four glucose tablets next and popped them into my mouth, one after the other. Then, to keep my mind occupied so it wouldn't send me spiraling into hysteria worrying about Dad, I decided to read. With the shelter of the tree and the aid of my headlamp, I had just enough light to make out the words on the page.

January 27th, 1945

Dear Mom and Pop,

Italy is in ruins. You wouldn't believe how much destruction the Germans left in their path. Buildings are in crumbles, broken-down tanks litter the roads, and the people are suffering. The Nazis have formed a Winter Line across a series of ridges in this moun- tainous part of Italy. They have the high ground, but this is what the fellas and I have been training for. Most of us are bone tired, dirty, and unshaven, but we are willing and ready to fulfill our mission. I must be careful what I say now that I'm at the front lines in case one of my letters fell into the enemy's hands. What I can tell you is that I spend hours at a time in a foxhole with the rumble of ammunition overhead, and it is the idea of Sunday breakfasts at home—stacks and stacks of pancakes, sausage, and warm maple syrup—that gets me through the darkest times.

Your loving son,

Will

I must've drifted off while I was reading. When I woke, it took a moment for me to realize that the howling I heard wasn't the wind, it was Molly, and she was pawing at my leg again. My stomach lurched. I didn't know how long it had been since I last tested. I immediately withdrew my kit and felt jittery as I pricked my finger with the lancet and got a reading. Even though it was a pretty fast process, the wait was awful. I didn't know what I'd do if I needed another shot of insulin. It was one thing to prick your finger, and another thing to insert a needle into your body. Despite the pressure from my parents and Dr. Morlock, I just hadn't been able to muster the courage.

I took a deep breath as I slipped the strip into the meter, and then let out a huge whoosh of air when my levels came back normal. It must've been everything else that had Molly so alarmed, not my blood sugar.

I ran my mittened hand down her back, mostly to soothe her, but it soothed me, too. She stared at me with her big brown eyes, then nestled her head close to my body. I listened to the storm. I couldn't tell if it was wishful thinking or the wind really sounded like it was dying down. Luckily, it turned out to be the latter.

The whiteout ended almost as swiftly as it began. Snowflakes still danced in the sky, but when I peered through the branches, I could see much farther than before. My heart swelled with hope. Maybe now I could find Dad. But with Molly pressed against me in the small space, I couldn't go anywhere. I unclipped her leash. "Go on," I commanded. Once she'd backed her way out, I scooted myself forward until I was no longer under the tree and the cover of the branches.

Molly darted around nervously while I used my pole to clear snow from the bottom of my boots and then clicked back into my ski bindings. "I know, Molly," I said. "I'm worried about Dad, too."

I was in such a rush, I didn't bother with her leash. Without being able to see a thing before, I'd been worried about finding my way back to where Dad had disappeared. Apparently, that wasn't an issue for Molly. She led the way, kicking freshly fallen snow up behind her as she dashed to the ridgeline ahead.

Once we got close, I removed my skis and drove them upright into the snow. I knew I'd be more comfortable creeping close to the edge without them. My heart was pounding so quickly by the time I reached the drop-off, I could hardly bear to look.

At last, I took a deep breath and peered over. What I saw was both better and worse than anything I'd hoped for. The face of the bluff was rocky, and branches were poking out everywhere. That was the bad news. The good news was that the drop-off wasn't an endless cliff. I didn't know the exact spot where Dad had gone over the edge, but at some places, it was only thirty feet or so to a pile of billowy snow.

"Dad!" I screamed, and my stomach clenched when there wasn't a reply.

I lowered myself to my hands and knees, trying to get a better view. Because of the angle and the branches, it was difficult to see anything directly beneath the drop-off. Molly trotted along the ridge. Her ears were perked and the black tufts of fur on her back were raised. She was on high alert.

"What is it?" I asked. "Did you hear something?"

She whined nervously and I called out to Dad once more, as loud as I could.

"Emily?" This time, I thought I heard my name being called, but it was so faint I feared I had imagined it. But then Dad's voice rang again. "Em, are you there?"

It sounded frighteningly weak and raw, but also so very sweet. I nearly broke into tears, knowing he was still alive.

"Are you okay?" I called down.

The silence just about killed me. *Please, God, please let him be okay,* my heart pleaded to the heavens. "Dad?" I choked as I spilled out his name.

He paused for so long, I thought he might never answer. When his reply did come at last, it was far from what I wanted to hear.

"I'm hurt pretty bad. It's my leg . . . There's no way I'm going to be able to ski out of here." He sounded so strained and despondent that it sent shivers throughout my body. A tightness wrapped itself around my rib cage, preventing me from gulping in the air I desperately needed. Dad was hurt. He was alive, but he was hurt. I knew him well enough to know that "pretty bad" was serious. He'd once shot a nail through his thumb while working on our deck and said it was "no big deal."

My legs went weak beneath me. I stumbled back a step. We were miles and miles away from civilization. If he couldn't ski out of here . . . *Oh, God, what was going to happen to us?*

Up until that moment, the idea that we might die in the wilderness had felt like a very distant, very small possibility. Like the way riding in a vehicle held the danger of a horrific car accident. Sure, it could happen, but no one ever really expected it would.

The idea that we might not make it out of the backcountry alive suddenly felt all too real, and I'd never been more terrified.

The fact that we were both quiet for a spell likely meant that Dad was as scared out of his mind as I was. I'd assumed that if something went terribly wrong in the backcountry, I would be the one who needed help. I thought Dad would have a plan for our survival. An overwhelming sense of weight and responsibility crashed down on me. I hadn't even considered that he might be the one who'd need rescuing.

I swallowed the bile rising in my throat. If Dad and I didn't come back, it would completely wreck Mom. I pushed her into letting me go, but I knew she'd still blame herself for not putting her foot down. She might never get over it. *No.* I shook my head. I couldn't let that happen. I had to find a way out of this mess, a way back to her. But I was drowning in doubt. It was too much. I wasn't comfortable taking care of myself in the wintery wilderness. How on earth was I going to get Dad and me both out alive?

CHAPTER 14

What do we do?" I could hear the panic in my voice as my words bounced off the rocks and were absorbed by the snow. I thought maybe Dad was just taking time to think through a solution. As time dragged on, I knew he hadn't heard me.

"Dad? Daaad?" I began pacing along the ridge as I continued yelling for my father's attention. Soon it was painfully clear that the question wasn't "What do we do," it was "What was I going to do?"

Whenever things got intense, I'd always had my parents or a coach by my side reminding me to stay calm, to keep my head in the game. Out here, with Dad unresponsive and no one else to turn to, my thoughts spiraled out of control.

Was Dad sleeping? Did he have a concussion? What if he never woke up? It was so cold. I had to do something, but what? What was I going to do? *What was I going to do?*

It was Molly that pulled me out of my rising hysteria. As she often did when I needed her, she leaned against my leg.

Her weight grounded me. I took a deep breath. The first thing I needed to do was think.

I didn't know what to do for Dad, so I needed to find someone who did. I dug my cell phone out of my inside jacket pocket. It had zero bars. Would Mom get worried if I missed too many of her texts or phone calls and send help? No, probably not. Not for several more days at least. It would be forever before anyone figured out that we were in trouble and came looking for us.

I really needed Dad's advice. He was the one with all the outdoor experience.

I tried calling down to him again, but it was no use.

The longer Molly and I stood at the ridge, the more distressed she became. I think she was feeding off my own anxious energy. I patted between her ears, trying to soothe her. She looked up at me and met my eyes. "I wish you could tell me what to do," I said. She cocked her head as if she was trying to understand me, then left my side.

"What are you doing?" I asked as she paced along the ridge like she was searching for something. Before I understood what was happening, she took a terrific leap right over the edge. My heart sprang into my throat. I bolted forward to get a better view. Fortunately, she'd picked a spot where the gradient wasn't quite as steep, and she carefully bounded from one rocky outcrop to the next.

"Molly!" Before I finished calling her name, she'd landed safely in the white powdery snow below.

Dad groaned, and my heart rejoiced. A sign of life! "Dad, can you hear me? Dad?"

Molly yipped in return, but Dad didn't speak.

"Oh, Molly, you dumb, loyal dog you." As much as I wanted her with me, I understood why she'd done it. She was trained to help, and Dad needed help. But I needed her, too, and I couldn't safely go down the way she had. I felt more alone than ever.

The wind started to howl again, and the gray, gray day began fading to black. Darkness came so early in the winter! The bluff provided some shelter for Dad and Molly, but I was completely exposed on the ridgeline. When I wasn't calling for them, my teeth were chattering, and everything felt numb, including my head. It was hard to think through my options while I was turning into a Popsicle. One thing was clear: If I didn't get out of the cold soon, I wouldn't be in any shape to get Dad the help he needed.

"Keep him warm!" I called to Molly, but it's not like that was a command she was trained to follow. I could only hope instinct would keep her snuggled close to his side.

We'd had cell service at the last hut, but I didn't think it was smart to backtrack at this point. It had taken the better part of the day to make it here. It would soon be pitch-black. Even in daylight, everything would look different coming from the opposite direction. I didn't trust myself to find it and I couldn't afford to be wandering around with the freezing temperatures in the dark.

The next hut was a gamble. I didn't know if there would be service or not, but at least I knew I was fairly close. "Less than an hour," Dad had said before things went sideways. It felt like a lifetime ago, but it was still true. The next hut was less than an hour away. If I got moving, I might make it there while I still had some light to navigate by.

I hadn't gotten a good look at the route we were taking on Dad's phone, but I had peered over Dad's shoulder at the map he'd printed out the night before. We'd taken the ridge-line because of the risk of avalanches instead of the easier trail through the valley.

If I stayed on higher ground, I thought at some point I'd see the hut down below. I gathered all my courage, dug out my headlamp, knowing I'd need it in the dimming light, and set out along the ridge. To keep my mind off leaving Dad and Molly behind, I thought of Will and the other ski troopers and all they had endured. They trained to face the harshest conditions. They might have even skied along this very mountain.

It made me feel not quite as alone to know that they had survived these surroundings and gone on to fight bigger battles. I gave myself a pep talk. I wasn't a soldier, but I was fit, and I was brave. I could do this!

An hour later I was colder than ever, and my headlamp was only cutting the darkness less than halfway down to the bottom of the valley. Even then, thickets of branches and trees were swallowing up what little light I was putting out. I was convinced I was going to pass the hut if I hadn't already, and my confidence was entirely deflated. Who had I been kidding? I couldn't do this. Not in a million years.

But . . . Dad! Molly! I had to go on. I had to reach someone who could help us.

I stopped in my tracks and shivered in the wind while I debated skiing down to a lower elevation. I didn't know if it would be easier or harder to find the hut if I was down in the valley. Really, there was a good chance I'd miss it either way. And honestly, apart from the higher avalanche risk, I was afraid to enter the wooded basin alone, and at night. I thought of the wolves and a quiver ran down my spine.

No, I needed to stay on the high ground for as long as possible. I also needed to stay alert and watch for any signs of people or trails leading to the hut.

I turned my head side to side, shining my light as far as I could see. The glow sliced through twisted tree branches and cast long, strange shadows on the snow. In open areas the beam grew wider until it was chopped off by the darkened night. As I scanned, a flicker caught my attention. I almost missed it. I shined my headlamp back where I thought it had come from, in a dense area of the forest below. As soon as my beam hit the same exact spot, a small, almost imperceptible light glimmered back once more.

"Hello!" I called out. "Is anyone there?"

No answer. That seemed to be a common theme lately. Me crying out and the universe staying silent.

"Please! I need help!" I tried again. And, again, nothing.

Still, I wasn't ready to give up on the only sign of, well, anything I'd seen in miles. I made a split-second decision, turned my skis downhill, and shot after the only other source of brightness for as far as I could see. My route was open for several hundred feet before I neared the tree line.

Now that the sun had gone down, a thin layer of ice had formed. My skis were scraping against the snow one moment, and I was sliding out of control the next. I'd been in such a rush to get to the light, fearing it was other travelers that would be gone before I reached them, that I hadn't paid attention to the dark, slick areas in front of me. My heart skipped a beat as I careened toward a tree, unable to slow my speed or find any traction.

The evergreen was as wide as a car and as tall as a bus. I thought to myself, *This is how skiers die or at least wind up in the hospital.* There was nothing I could do to prevent the collision, and then . . . there was.

My left ski ran across a softer patch of snow. I pivoted immediately. I couldn't stop, but it was enough to shift my direction slightly. Instead of running head on into the trunk, pine needles lashed my face, scratched across my goggles, belted my outer layers, and at last, slowed my progress enough that I regained control.

I breathed heavily but knew I had no time to waste on recovery. I could no longer see the light and I had to catch whoever had shined it. "Wait!" I cried again as soon as I'd caught my breath. "Wait! I need help!"

I skied like my life depended on it, because maybe it did. Dad's and Molly's, too. I knew I was zipping in and out of the trees too quickly, but I had no choice but to go as fast as I could. When I reached the spot where I'd seen the glimmer, no one was there. I whipped my head around, looking for tracks in the snow. Whoever had shined the light couldn't have gone that far. I could still find them. I could find someone to help.

But . . .

Other than my tracks, all I could see was smooth, untouched snow all around me. It didn't make sense. And then, I looked up.

In the beam from my headlamp, I caught an arrow and a reflector the size of a quarter just above it. It was a trail blaze, and I was immensely lucky that I'd caught it with my headlamp from so far away. Still, I was devastated. It had been a day of loss and agony. The glimmer had been something for me to cling to, a literal and figurative ray of light. Yet I was right back where I started. Helpless and alone. With each new blow, it was getting harder and harder to imagine that I'd ever claw my way out of the darkness.

CHAPTER 15

By the time I reached Pine Valley Hut, I was so cold and exhausted that my body was stiff, and I ached from my forehead to my pinky toes. It crossed my mind that Dad would've been proud of me for making it this far. I'd successfully followed the trail blazes, not missing a one since I'd shined my headlamp on the first reflector. However, proving myself seemed of little importance at the moment. All I wanted now was to find someone who could help us make it out of the backcountry alive.

I held my breath as I pushed through the door, all while clinging to a shred of hope that I'd find another group here. No matter that the snow was piled high and undisturbed on the front porch. The wind could've picked up *after* the travelers went inside, I reasoned.

"Hello?" I called out as soon as I took one step into the foyer. I would've given anything to bump into Ahmad, Chloe, Dan, or anyone else for that matter. "Is anyone here?" I tried again.

Not only was there no response, but the hut was also

cold, and it felt empty. Because it *was* empty. The air was so stale and musty, I could practically taste my disappointment.

The wind gusted in behind me, swirling flakes across the wood floor. I took deep breaths to calm myself. Okay, no one was here, but maybe I had service. Now that I had shelter, I could check. I removed my gloves and whipped out my phone, but the screen was black. I pressed the home button, then I jammed the on-off button with my thumb. Great. Not only was there no one here, it didn't matter whether there was service or not. My phone was completely dead. There was no electricity in the huts, only wood-burning stoves and solar-powered lights. And Dad had the extra battery pack.

I slumped to the floor and kicked the door shut behind me.

The chill of the wooden planks seeped through my clothing. I needed a new plan. But all I could do was lie there and sulk.

The thing that finally got me off the floor was the same thing that had landed me there—the realization that there was no one to turn to. It was me, and me alone, who had to figure a way out of this nightmare. I rose to my feet, reopened the door, and stared out into the frigid darkness.

Part of me wanted to run straight back to Dad. Maybe he was awake now? But even if he was, that didn't change the fact that he was too injured to ski. And in my current condition, there was no way I'd be able to move him.

On a flight I took to an out-of-state tournament, one where I actually paid attention to the flight attendant, I'd heard her say that in case of emergency, "put on your own oxygen mask before helping others." Honestly, I thought it sounded kinda selfish, at first. But it made sense. If you ran out of oxygen, you wouldn't be any use to anyone else. You couldn't rescue others when you needed rescuing.

If I went back out in the wind and the cold now, with my levels who-knew-where and Molly not around to alert me, I might be done for before I ever reached Dad. One of his favorite sayings was "Set yourself up for success." If I took care of myself and planned ahead, I might just have a chance. I shut the door again.

I wasn't dizzy or anything, but I was freezing. So I decided to build a fire before I did anything else. This wood-burning stove was identical to the ones in the other two huts. I'd watched Dad build fires in both. It hadn't looked hard and everything I needed was right there. I dove in, and . . . lighting the fire wasn't hard, but I forgot an important step. I didn't check to be sure the flue was open.

Smoke engulfed me. I choked and coughed as I reeled back, only to lunge forward a second later to pull the damper handle on the chimney. When I could breathe again, I discovered I was light-headed. I just wasn't sure if it was from inhaling too much smoke or having too much sugar in my blood.

I sat on the floor in front of the stove and dug out my testing kit while the fire warmed me. Even before my reading came back in the normal range, my head started to clear. It was a relief, but also a reminder. I took a bolus of insulin before dinner every night. Of course, my regular dinnertime passed hours ago. My stomach growled as if on cue.

Dr. Morlock said it wasn't the end of the world if I occasionally missed a shot. I'd taken an injection of long-acting insulin that morning. It would maintain a small amount of insulin in my system for nearly twenty-four hours. With my phone dead, I didn't know the exact time, but I knew sunrise was still a ways off. I needed to catch up as soon as possible, though, or my body would really get thrown out of whack. As much as I wanted to crawl into bed and sleep for all of eternity, I had to find my way back to Dad soon. For more reasons than one.

As I began to thaw, I hoped Molly's body heat would be enough for Dad. That or he'd been able to use the emergency items in his pack. It hit me that I might be able to use my avalanche beacon to connect with Dad, since he had one, too.

I whipped out my transceiver. Dad and I had done some training with them on our day trip. I switched mine from tracking to search mode, praying for a signal. The thing was, as much as I wanted the beep-beep-beep noise to indicate that he was near, it would've taken a miracle. At this point, I was way out of range.

It would be helpful, though, if I had trouble locating him again, and I was glad I'd remembered how to change modes. I dug through my pack, looking for anything else that might be helpful. I'd held on to the topographic map when Dad had me navigate to the previous hut. I was thankful he had. I examined it again, more closely this time, looking for places along the ridge where the lines spread farther apart. There wasn't any one area that appeared to be a slam dunk. There were a few spots that didn't seem as steep, though . . . I only hoped I could find one of them in the dark.

After I finished studying the map, I melted snow on the stove and refilled my hydration pack. Then I rummaged through every single cabinet in the hut, searching for things that might be useful on my rescue mission. The problem was, what we needed the most and what the hut could provide, I couldn't take with me. Shelter. As difficult as it would be to head back into the cold, dark night, I would have to summon the courage. Something told me that everything

I'd been through so far was only the beginning. What I faced next would be harder than any challenge I'd been through before. And maybe you could pick some of your battles, but this one felt like another one where I didn't have a choice.

CHAPTER 16

I f this had happened a year ago, I knew what Dad would tell me to do. He'd want me to forget about his comfort and safety and stay put while waiting for help to arrive. It would've been the sensible thing, but I wondered if I could've lived with the guilt as time ticked by.

Now, even if I somehow convinced myself it was okay to leave Dad and Molly out in the elements while I holed up in the hut, it wasn't an option. I needed Dad to give me my shots. Plus, he had the majority of my insulin in his pack. I had to go back for him *and* my medication.

I gathered myself and my stuff. I wouldn't say I felt strong, or brave, or reenergized as I left the warmth of the hut behind. But I didn't have second thoughts about it. I guess you could say I was resolved about the matter by then. I was ready to do what needed to be done, and that was a big change from when I'd arrived hoping to find someone to get me and Dad out of this awful predicament.

The snow had completely tapered off, and with the wind mellowed to a gentle breeze, it was easy to retrace my tracks.

With the aid of my skins, I was able to slowly make my way through the forest and back up the considerable incline following the two parallel indentions in the snow.

The hour's journey back to the place Dad had fallen and Molly had leaped over the edge passed more quickly now that I knew where I was heading. I was laser focused on my return, but now that the night was still, and a crescent moon was peeking out from behind the clouds, I could appreciate the beauty of nature again. A violent storm had barreled through, but you'd never know it if you hadn't been in it. Sure, the snow had deepened and shifted from one drift to the next, but everything was so peaceful. It was like an entirely different world from the one that had ripped me and Dad apart.

Once I reached the edge, I took a deep breath and shouted. My voice carried farther when it didn't have to compete with the wind. "Dad! Molly!"

I was getting used to there being no response, so when Molly whined excitedly, I was only half disappointed.

"Good girl," I called down. "Is . . . is Dad okay?"

"Woof." I took that as a yes, because my heart couldn't bear any other answer.

"I'm going to come down there," I yelled, still having a conversation with my dog.

"Woof!"

It was probably for the best that I couldn't tell Dad what I had in mind. He'd only try to talk me out of it. He was all a-life-without-risk-isn't-worth-living when it came to himself, but I knew he'd be more cautious when it was my life on the line. He'd say it was too dangerous. Maybe it was, but the way I saw it, there weren't any risk-free options at this point.

If I'd read the scale on the map correctly, the spot I was looking for was about half a mile farther down the ridgeline. Skiing in the dark was almost as bad as skiing through a blizzard, at least in terms of being able to see what lay on the other side of the ridge. Dad's GPS would've been really helpful in determining how far I'd skied. I knew I could ski about ten miles per hour. That meant it should only take me three minutes to reach the gentler slope I thought I'd found on the map. When I'd been skiing for a bit longer—ten? fifteen minutes? I wasn't sure—I decided I'd passed it and that I needed to turn around.

This time, heading back toward where I'd left Molly and Dad, my headlamp illuminated a place I thought might be skiable. It definitely wasn't a gentle slope, but the ground beneath rose closer to the ridgeline. It was only a fifteen-foot drop or so. Everywhere else appeared double that. As I examined more closely, one spot in particular looked promising—a place with a bit of an overhang and no obstacles in my path. A place where the ground below was sloping in the right direction.

I tried not to think about what I was about to do because I didn't want to psych myself out. I'd skied off jumps in the terrain park hundreds of times. I'd always been more into speed than tricks while downhill skiing. Still, some of the jumps I hit had been at least fifteen feet high. This wasn't that much different. Was it? I swallowed hard.

I dug my poles in and built up speed. I popped my legs at just the right moment, and I was airborne. The sensation of flying took my breath away. My momentum carried me safely over the lip before gravity caught up with me. I bent my legs to absorb the impact, then turned both skis parallel. I went down hard and skidded to a stop on my side. It wasn't pretty, but I'd made it.

Without delay, I bounced back to my feet and was on my way. I'd left the avalanche beacon on, but Molly came running as soon as she saw me. Which was sooner than I saw her—she blended in with the night—and before the beacon picked up Dad's signal. She ran circles around me, wagging her tail as I skied straight for Dad and the beeps grew louder.

I didn't mean to ignore her. I was thrilled to be reunited. I was just more worried about my father. He was lying still, his body splayed across the snow.

I clicked out of my skis. "Please be alive," I whispered under my breath as I drew close.

I bent over beside him and gently shook his arm. "Dad?"

He didn't tense. He didn't react in any way. The way his arm jiggled freely terrified me. I tried again, speaking his name louder and shaking harder.

At last, something . . . my voice, my touch, or my light shining on his face must've brought him back to awareness, because he rolled his head toward me and moaned. His skin was pale, his eyes were glassy, and his goggles were half hanging off his head. That his goggles were askew wasn't the alarming part. The alarming part was that he hadn't bothered to fix them. He was pretty much in a heap where he'd fallen. It must've hurt him too much to move. But he *was* moving.

"Dad," I said. Tears of relief pooled in my eyes as he blinked back his own. I didn't like how he was shivering, so I immediately pulled out my survival kit, and then draped the blanket over his torso.

"What are we going to do?" I asked.

"Hmmm," Dad responded. Molly returned to his side. His eyes fell shut for a beat too long, but they fluttered open when she licked his forehead. Still, his glazed-over expression made me wonder if he'd hit his head on the way down. Or else he was delirious with pain. I started checking him over.

There didn't appear to be any blood, thank goodness. But one look at his lower limbs and alarm bells went off in my head. His knee wasn't the only bend in his right leg.

My heart screamed at me to get Dad out of here pronto. He needed a hospital. I knew it wasn't that simple, though. I had to stay calm and think. In one of his letters, Will had said the keys to surviving injury in the backcountry were, in order: stabilize, shelter, water, fire, and signaling.

Before Dad was going anywhere, I had to do something about his leg. I hopped to my feet and began scrounging around for something to create a splint. Problem was, there was nothing but powder all around us. My eyes wandered up and down and the beam from my headlamp bounced off bare, rocky ledges. Then, just beneath the cliff, I caught a glimpse of something plastic sticking out of the snow. It was almost entirely buried, but I recognized it as the handle to one of Dad's ski poles. It would work perfectly for a splint—that was, if I could find something to secure it with.

As I rifled through my pack, the bright orange paracord bracelet around my wrist caught my attention. I could unravel it . . . The cord was strong, but it was also thin. I worried it would be uncomfortable for Dad. I kept looking.

My fingers caught hold of one end of my scarf. Unlike the paracord, it was thick and soft. I let my pack fall to the ground and the scarf pulled free, like silks from a magician's sleeve. Within minutes I had the pole, I had my scarf, and I was getting ready to strap it to Dad's bad leg.

That's when he wheezingly said, "It needs to be realigned first." It was the first comprehensible thing he'd said since I'd arrived. If he'd gathered the strength to mention it, it had to be important. I'd seen broken bones get reset in movies before, but I wasn't a doctor, and it wasn't something I'd ever imagined myself doing. It wasn't something I thought I was *capable* of doing. I shook my head.

Dad held my eyes. Without saying another word, he told me it was essential.

I dropped my chin. "Okay," I conceded, but I had no idea where to start. I eyed the crookedness of his leg, bewildered and afraid.

"Traction . . ." he said. "Push with one hand . . . Pull with the other."

I nodded even though I still didn't know what I was doing, then I gripped above and below the fracture.

"Good," he said weakly. Without giving me time to ask questions or prepare, he sputtered "Go!" and then gritted his teeth.

With my left hand below the crooked bend in his leg, I pulled. With my right hand above it, I pushed.

Dad yelped in pain. "Don't stop," he cried through his clenched mouth. Color drained from his already pale face, and his eyes betrayed his anguish.

Doubt washed over me. I wasn't strong enough. It had been the longest day of my life, and I was spent. My grip loosened, but my dad's pleading expression told me I couldn't give up. Not yet.

I repositioned my fingers and dug deep. I silenced the voices in my head telling me I was sick and weak, and pulled with all my might. Miraculously, the bone aligned. His leg was straight once more. He breathed heavily as if he'd just finished running a marathon. His eyes fell closed again.

I didn't waste any more time. Using the pocketknife from my survival kit, I cut my plaid scarf into long, thin strips. One strip at a time, I secured the pole to the outside of Dad's broken leg, then I tied his legs together for added support. It wasn't pretty. The scarf was frayed, and my knots were sloppy. But it did the trick. I could mark "stabilize" off my list. Which meant it was time to move on to shelter.

Looping my arms under Dad's and across his chest, I dragged him to a position closer to the cliff face. It wasn't the best cover, but between the emergency blanket and being out of the wind, I knew he'd at least be warmer here than where I'd found him.

"I'll be back," I said. "I'm going to go find us some better shelter."

The temps would drop even lower as the night went on. Dad was miserable enough. It'd be far worse for both of us if we spent hours out in the cold and dark.

Molly seemed torn between staying with Dad and going with me. She waited a bit with him before catching up. "Thanks," I said, and she wagged her tail. I was doing my best to be brave and take charge of this terrible situation. It was easier, though, when I didn't have to do it all alone.

I skied along the base of the bluff first, looking for a way back up to the ridge. Returning to the Pine Valley hut with him would be ideal. We could set up camp there until another party arrived. It was a popular route, and with the blizzard over, more skiers would be coming soon. If I could only find an easy way to ascend . . . To be honest, I knew it was a long shot before I started looking, since I'd studied the map and knew exactly where the gentlest gradient was located. I might've been able to scale the bluff where I'd skied down. But with Dad and his leg, there wasn't any way it would be manageable for him.

I extended my search out and away from the ridge. Occasionally, I glanced back to be sure I didn't lose sight of it. We had to return to Dad, and I didn't want to be gone too long. I was looking for a place to dig out a snow cave, or a fallen tree like the one I'd waited out the storm beneath. What I found was even better.

At first glance, I thought it was a tight cluster of trees within the forest. As I came nearer, I realized it was a small, abandoned cabin. The entire structure was about the size of my bedroom, and the wooden planks that I'd mistaken for trees were leaning to one side. Some of them had fallen and there was a hole the size of a cantaloupe in the snow-covered roof. Most likely, it had been built by hunters decades ago. It was the type of place my parents would've told me to steer clear of under normal circumstances for fear of collapse or tetanus from a rusty nail. The threat from the cold and wind trumped both of those.

I tried the front door, but it was blocked by snow. Dad had the avalanche shovel in his pack, so I improvised. I found a flat board nearby (probably a roof piece that had been blown off by the wind) and used it to dig a path. Once I could swing the door open, it nearly fell off the hinges. The cabin was dark and smelled dank inside. There was a small metal bedframe, but something, probably rodents, had ripped the mattress and bedding to shreds.

I scanned the tiny cabin, and my eyes landed on the one thing we needed almost as much as shelter—a place to build a fire. Molly had followed me inside. I turned to her, and she must've read the relief on my face because she did a small play bow before springing a few inches into the air. I smiled. "Yep, let's go get Dad."

Dad was barely coherent when I returned. Still, I tried helping him rise to his feet. It was too painful for him. Not to mention it would be impossible for him to make any progress in the deep snow with his legs tethered together for support.

I kicked myself for even trying. It was a waste of energy—a precious commodity for both of us at the moment. After helping him back to the ground, I tried wrapping my arms under his and pulling from behind. I was exhausted by the time we'd moved two feet. I'd left my pack and skis at the cabin, but I wasn't strong enough to carry his pack and pull him at the same time.

"Work smarter, not harder" is what I imagined Dad would say if he felt up to talking. There had to be a better way.

I stopped a minute to think. In one of Will's letters, he'd talked about going hunting with the guys in his platoon. They'd dragged their kill out of the forest in tarps. I knew Dad had one packed in his emergency kit.

I rummaged through Dad's pack. The tarp was folded neatly at the very bottom. Careful not to lose anything, I worked it out from beneath the other items before spreading it over the snow. Then, with a little help from Dad, I slid him on top. Testing his weight as I tugged on the tarp, I decided it was doable, but just barely. I'd have to come back later for his stuff.

The cabin was about the length of two football fields away from the bluff. I could've sprinted the distance in less than a few minutes. That is, if there wasn't deep snow, boulders, and trees in the way. And if I wasn't trying to lug someone nearly double my weight along with me. It didn't help that my energy levels were dropping. Finding Dad, and then somewhere to shelter, had boosted my adrenaline, but the stress of it all was starting to catch up with me. At least, I hoped that's all it was.

Inch by inch, I dragged Dad across the snow. The tarp reduced the amount of resistance. It made things easier, for sure. But that didn't mean it wasn't hard. I was tired and every time I hit a hard clump of snow or uneven ground and it jostled his legs, he winced and moaned. Molly darted in and out of the trees around us. I knew she wanted us to move faster, but I was going as fast as I could possibly manage.

At last, we arrived. Molly pushed the door to the cabin open ahead of us. I dragged Dad inside and then collapsed on the floor next to him.

CHAPTER 17

February 19th, 1945

Dear Mom and Pop,

You might have already heard the news that we took Vista Ridge yesterday. The Germans thought it would be impossible, even in the daylight. We scaled it at night, using five different routes. The route I took was a sheer rock wall and required a rope to ascend. There were seven hundred of us in all, and we pushed over the ridge while the Germans were eating breakfast. A fella named Albert was shot right in the chest by the enemy as we surprised their camp, but the bullet deflected off a prayer book and harmonica in his pocket. Can you believe it? Not everyone was so lucky as we drove the Germans back. It was a huge victory. Still, I can't help but think of how far we still have to go. Vista

Ridge is only one of many ridges and I've seen so much cold, death, and hunger already. It feels like this war will never end.

Your loving son,

Will

There was so much still to do, but I couldn't. I had to rest. It seemed like an odd time to read, but I felt connected to Will in a way that was hard to explain. He felt like a friend. Even a brief glimpse into his life and struggles gave me strength the same way a pat on the back from a teammate did. Still, the wind blowing through the cracks in the boards and in through the ceiling was bone-chilling. Minutes after I'd crumpled to the floor, I was back on my feet. Dad and I were both shivering. I hugged my arms to my chest and peered around the room in the dim light. Unlike the huts, it was clear no one else had been to this cabin in ages. The chances of someone happening by in the dead of winter had to be zero to none.

We needed to figure out our options, but Dad was in no shape to plan. He'd been out in the cold for too long. I had to warm him up! Thankfully, a bin by the fireplace was half-filled with kindling and logs. It was caked in dust and must've been there for decades, but it was dry and would still burn. I had matches in my emergency kit. I double-checked that the flue was open—I didn't want to make that mistake again! Then, after a few failing strikes, I managed to start a fire.

I pulled my blanket up around Dad's shoulders and tried to make him as comfortable as possible before joining him on the floor once more. His eyes were closed. I didn't know if he was sleeping or trying to shield himself from the pain. I decided not to bother him just yet. It crossed my mind that I needed to go back for his pack, and that now would be a good time. But I was still too exhausted from having dragged him all the way here. *I'll rest just a few more minutes*, I told myself. *Then I'll go.*

Next thing I knew, Molly was whining and pawing at my leg. My eyelids felt like lead as I forced them open. My mouth felt like I'd woken up sucking on a cotton ball. The cabin was completely dark except for the glowing orange of the flames.

It was the middle of the night. I'd skipped dinner and my injection. I hadn't checked my levels for hours. My body needed fuel and, no doubt, insulin.

"Dad." I shook his shoulder.

He groaned. In the firelight, I could see his eyelids flicker open, then closed again. He was in pain. He needed sleep.

I worried my lip, not sure what to do. I wanted him to rest, but was it even more important that I got an injection? Probably. Molly tracked me with her eyes. She pawed my leg a second time. My head felt fuzzy. My thoughts were like billowy clouds.

"I know, girl." I'd gone too long without carbs. The meal Dad had planned for at the hut was no longer a possibility. I knew he'd also packed charcuterie—cured meats, cheeses, nuts, and dried fruit—in case we'd arrived late and there wasn't time to cook. But that was all in his pack. The pack I hadn't yet retrieved.

I took a sip from my hydration hose. Bone dry.

Stabilize. Shelter. Water. Fire. Signaling.

I'd skipped a step. Panic crept back into my chest. All at once, everything seemed too overwhelming. I needed insulin. I needed water. I needed food. There wasn't an easy solution for any of them. My head was swirling. I took slow, deep breaths to calm myself.

"One crisis at a time," I said to Molly as I pulled out my kit.

The thrumming I felt inside was similar to what I'd felt when Dr. Morlock first explained to me what living with diabetes was going to be like. I didn't think I'd ever be able to handle any of it. It was too much to take in at once. But little by little, I had. That is, everything but actually inserting the needle. The thrumming intensified.

"One step at a time," I told myself. If I dwelled on the fact that I was scared to give myself a shot, I'd never come close to accomplishing what needed to be done. Still, I struggled to even overcome the easy part—the calculation. I'd need to eat within fifteen minutes of giving myself a bolus of insulin. Problem was, I didn't have Dad's pack yet, so I didn't know what I was going to eat. But my body needed fuel now.

Thrum, thrum, thrum went the base of my neck. Then I remembered that Mom had stashed a bag of energy bites in Molly's pack. It wasn't quite dinner, but they were better than the minimal amount of trail food I had left in my pack.

I calculated what I thought was enough for three energy bites. I prepped the pen and twisted the appropriate number of clicks as I'd seen Mom, Dad, or the school nurse do hundreds of times. Then it was on to the hard part.

Molly watched me intently. She cocked her head. "I'm getting there," I said, peeling layer upon layer of clothing until my bare belly was poking out. For some reason, though, I couldn't stand the idea of sticking myself in the stomach. I held the pen above my skin, but I just couldn't do it.

Molly's ears drooped as I pulled back my hand.

"Gee, thanks," I said. "Like I wasn't disappointed in myself enough already."

My stomach wasn't my only option, though. I thought maybe, just maybe, I could manage my upper thigh.

I undid the button on my pants, slid them down along with my long underwear, and positioned the injection pen above the fleshiest part of my leg. Next, I pinched my skin with my other hand before turning my head away. I took a deep breath, but I still couldn't bring myself to inject the needle and press down on the dose knob. Then Molly moved closer. She nudged me with her nose, and I felt stronger.

"Okay," I said. "I know. I have to do this." This time, before I could chicken out, I curled my fingers tighter around the pen, inserted the needle, ignored the painful prick in my leg, and then depressed the knob. When I was finished administering the dose, I pulled the needle straight out. A gush of air escaped my lungs with it. A part of me wished Mom and Dad could've seen me. A larger part was proud of me for finally accomplishing this all on my own.

I tore into Molly's pack. Along with the energy bites, I found a baggie of sugar cubes. It felt like a much-needed hug from Mom, knowing she'd secretly stashed them there. My throat was dry, and the energy bites were hard to swallow, but I gobbled them down anyway.

Next, water. There was an abundance of snow. I had fire to melt it. What I didn't have was a pot. I scrounged around in the shadows, looking for something to use. I didn't find any pots or pans, but there was an old cast iron skillet with a lid. I cleaned it as best I could with my mittened hand, scraping out the dirt and grime and dumping it on the hardwood floor. I smiled to myself, thinking how mortified Mom would be if I did that at home. When I was more or less satisfied that whatever remained in the skillet wasn't going to kill me if I ingested a little of it, I took the skillet outside, found the cleanest snow around—in a mound a few feet from the cabin—and scooped up a small amount.

I brought the skillet back inside and laid it on a grate above the fire. I made several more trips outdoors and returned with handfuls of snow to add to the skillet. Little by little the snow turned into boiling water. It was a clunkier, less efficient process than it had been at the huts, but it worked just the same.

The heat from the skillet handle warmed my hand through my mitten when I removed it from the fire and set it aside to cool. My throat was parched, so I waited just long enough to be sure the water wouldn't burn me or melt my hydration pack before opening it up and pouring it inside. I sipped warmish water through the hose, relieving my thirst.

I'd left a small amount of water in the skillet for Molly. She lapped it up. Then, as I hand-fed her dog food from her saddlebag, Dad stirred awake. I offered him a sip from my hydration pack. He rose to his elbows and greedily sucked it dry. While he ate a few of the energy bites, I started the process of melting snow in the skillet all over again.

"I can't believe you did all this," Dad said. Maybe it was

the glow of the fire, but it seemed some of the color had returned to his face.

It was a huge relief to hear him speak and to see some life coming back into him. I had a billion questions to ask, starting with "What now?" but I didn't want to press too hard. I didn't want to stress him out just when he was starting to show some improvement. And, yeah, a small part of me still wanted to impress him.

"Thanks. I need to go back for your pack," I said, thinking it would go a step further in proving how capable I was.

"In the dark? I don't know if that's such a good idea."

He was right to be worried. "I know the way. I'll take Molly with me. I have a headlamp . . ." Then I said one of the things that was weighing heaviest on my chest. "My extra insulin is in your pack." Now that we were off our planned route and Dad couldn't ski, I didn't know how many days we'd be stuck in the backcountry.

Dad's eyes shot back to mine. "I can't believe I didn't think of that." He nodded gravely. In the pause that followed, I knew we were both questioning how well his mind was working after such a terrible fall. It had to have rattled him good. "You're right," he said. "It can't wait until morning."

As the cabin had warmed, I'd shed my shell layers. I started slipping them back on.

"You really are amazing, kiddo," Dad added. "Not many thirteen-year-olds could've pulled off what you did today."

"Thanks, Dad." I stood a little taller.

"I mean it. I'm proud of you. I'm glad you inherited my athleticism, but even gladder you got your mother's grit and determination."

I stopped halfway through pulling on a mitten. Dad never said things like this. He was hardly ever sentimental, and I hadn't heard him say anything nice about Mom in a long time.

His words gave me just the boost of confidence I needed. With my chin held high, I said, "I shouldn't be gone too long." I finished pulling on the gear I'd worn earlier. But I waited until Molly and I were outside the cabin to flick on the headlamp strapped around my wool hat.

The temperature had dropped significantly. I shivered as I turned my head, cut the darkness with my headlamp, and examined the wintery forest. Drifts of snow. Shadows. Lots and lots of trees. Branches reached into the sky like a complex network of arteries and blood vessels. With the gentle wind, the forest seemed to pulse a rhythmic heartbeat. Everything seemed calm and peaceful now, but who knew what dangers lurked beyond my narrow beam of light?

Ever since the raging storm, I'd been through one suffocating bout of fear after another. I felt the need to suck in as much frigid night air as possible, even if the shock of cold made my lungs contract. I quickly strapped on my skis and set out. I was worried that Dad's pack would be too heavy for me to return with. The ground between the cabin and the bluff was relatively flat, though. If I could heave it onto my shoulders, I should be able to make it back. At least it was nowhere near the ninety-pound packs Will and the other ski soldiers trained with.

As I glided through the trees and the darkness, I started to feel better about things. Action felt good. We were in a tough situation, but we were working through it. Dad was in terrible pain, but he'd be okay. He was stabilized. We had shelter and water, and as soon as I retrieved Dad's pack, we'd have more food. Then Dad would figure out a way to signal for help. We would survive.

Molly seemed happier, too, as she dashed along beside me in the snow. The darkness felt thrilling instead of frightening and I felt lighter and lighter as I skied toward the bluff and Dad's pack.

I'm not sure what first tipped me off that something wasn't quite right: the way the hair stood up on Molly's back, or the empty wrapper lying on the fresh snow. As we reached the bluff, and the place where Dad had fallen, Molly began sniffing the air. Then she darted ahead. A low growl grumbled in her throat as she went.

I followed her with my eyes, all the way to Dad's pack and the contents strewn across the ground.

"No, no, no, no, no," I said as I increased my speed to catch up to Molly. She circled the area, sniffing wildly. I went straight for Dad's backpack to assess the damage. An animal, probably a fox or a pack rat, had torn into it, ripping the nylon to shreds. It had gone straight for the food. That was alarming enough. What was worse was that I couldn't find the insulated storage pack containing my extra insulin pens.

Frantic, I began crawling on the ground, searching the snow for the pack. It had to be there somewhere. I couldn't imagine that whatever creature had gotten into Dad's backpack would be very interested in it. Trail mix yes, but not pens full of insulin.

A few feet away, my glove connected with the rough canvas material. Relief poured in as I lifted the insulated storage pack from the snow, only to have it drain away just as quickly. There was a large rip in the top, it was halfway unzipped, and the pack was empty. The contents had spilled out. I glanced down and noticed the pens peeking out from the snow like little discharged arrows. Insulin, like water, freezes at around thirty-two degrees Fahrenheit. It was well below freezing now. With heart-thudding certainty, I knew all the extra insulin we'd packed was hopelessly ruined.

CHAPTER 18

I scavenged what I could from Dad's pack—a small amount of food that was still sealed and most of the survival gear—and returned to the cabin in a daze. When I pushed through the door, Dad rose on his elbows to greet me. His expectant smile made me crumble on the inside. And the outside, apparently, because when he saw the expression on my face, his also turned grave. "What is it?" he asked.

I shook my head, still not quite able to believe what had happened. "An animal. It . . . it got into your pack."

"Are you okay?" Dad asked.

"Yes, but . . ." I swallowed hard. "My extra insulin pens are gone."

Dad closed his eyes. He went so pale I thought he might faint. When his eyes fluttered open again, he asked, "How much do you have left?"

"Enough for one, maybe two more days." That was a best-case scenario, but I didn't tell him that.

"Then we'll just have to figure a way out of this mess before you run out," Dad said with forced optimism.

"Right," I said, and did my best to smile back.

I settled in beside him on the floor, and he helped me sort through the wreckage of his pack. The first aid kit was intact, and he immediately broke into the Tylenol.

"What about this?" I held up his avalanche beacon. It hadn't aided me much in locating him, but maybe he knew a way to use them to contact help that I didn't.

Dad shook his head. "They can only be used for close-range transmissions. Someone would have to be close by, actively searching for us, to pick up a signal."

Deflated, I dropped it back in the pile.

Next, we decided how to ration what little food we had left. Neither of us would eat anything more tonight than the energy bites we'd already had. Fortunately, the extra exercise of cross-country skiing had kept my sugar levels higher than normal. Most of the glucose tablets had been pilfered from Dad's pack. But I could use the sugar cubes Mom stashed in Molly's saddlebag for a quick pick-me-up, if needed.

Dad's GPS app was out of the question. The cold had zapped both of our phone batteries and the portable battery charger was completely drained. So we studied the topographic map, trying to determine our location. Even though I hoped I'd been wrong, Dad read it the same way I had. Scaling the bluff wasn't an option, and in his current condition, going around it to return to our original route would be nearly as impossible.

Dad pored over the map as though if he stared long enough, a solution would come to him. "Your mom won't know to send out a rescue crew for at least three more days. Normally, it's best to stay put and wait for help to arrive. But . . ." Dad let that thought go unfinished, like he didn't want to remind me that I couldn't wait three days. My body could go into diabetic ketoacidosis, or DKA, without insulin, which could be life-threatening. Going through everything had helped me keep my mind off the fact that my insulin supply had been greatly depleted. Panic bubbled up inside me again.

"If we forget about making it back to the huts, there might be a way to the highway from here," Dad went on. Then he sized me up as if trying to decide if I could drag him that far. We both knew I couldn't. "Tomorrow, when the sun comes up, do you think you can gather enough rocks to write HELP in giant letters in the snow? There's a treeless area near the bluff. Maybe we'll get lucky."

"Yeah, good idea," I said. I didn't like leaving our fate in the hands of luck, but what else was there to do?

"We have plenty of matches. We can burn fires to signal for help, too."

"Uh-huh," I said. We were deep in the backcountry; we'd

have to light the entire forest on fire to get someone's attention. Even if I was willing to go that far, there wasn't enough dry wood in the dead of winter to accomplish it. My mind kept leaping back to what he said about the highway. I couldn't drag him that far, but could I make it on my own?

"Dad," I said. "The highway—how many miles do you think it is from here?"

He studied my face in the firelight. "Out of the question," he said at last. "You're not making the trip alone. It's too dangerous."

"I wouldn't be on my own, not really. I'd have Molly," I countered.

"Molly won't help you steer clear of avalanches, or freezing temperatures, or wolves, or any number of things that could go wrong. We have food and shelter and water here. We have most everything we need."

"But not everything," I said sullenly.

"You're right. It's a gamble either way," Dad said.

"Then—"

Dad cut me off before I could finish making my point. If it was all a gamble, I thought we should at least try for the option that held a more promising outcome.

"No," Dad said firmly. "We stay together."

"But—"

He still wouldn't let me speak.

"No."

I stopped protesting, but on the inside, I was boiling with frustration. If he wasn't in such a weakened state, I would've fought harder to get my way. Still, despite his objections, I couldn't let it go. Not in my head, at least. Even with the fire lit, the holes in the cabin allowed too much cold to seep in. I shivered as I silently argued with him in my thoughts and failed to fall asleep.

I knew why he wanted me to stay. Setting out into the backcountry alone and finding my way to the highway seemed impossible. But sometimes, attempting the impossible was the best option. It had been for the Tenth Mountain Division when they scaled Vista Ridge. Staying at the bottom had to have seemed safer, just like staying with Dad felt safer. But in the long run, no action would've been more costly, for the ski soldiers and for me.

Dad said it was a gamble either way. But I thought it would be riskier not to try. If I waited here with Dad and no help came, we'd be out of options. He was worried that something might happen to me if I set out alone. If I didn't, we could both die. My window to decide was short. If I set out soon, I might have enough insulin to last until I found help. If I waited, I wouldn't.

I heard Dad moan.

"Dad," I whispered. "Are you awake?"

He groaned and grunted as he stirred but didn't answer.

I drew close to check on him. "Dad," I said again. His eyes half opened. "Amber?" he said, looking straight into my eyes. "I think the furnace is out. It's so cold."

I tried to keep my expression flat to hide how scared I felt. "It's okay," I said. "Go back to sleep." Amber was my mom's name. He was confused. I'd thought he was improving, but the pain and freezing temps were getting to him again.

Waiting, and watching our supplies run short while he was delirious with pain, and not being able to do anything about it would be unbearable. I knew then that I had to do something. I had to make another attempt to find help. It would be harder and farther than my trip to the Pine Valley hut, and this time, I couldn't fail.

CHAPTER 19

O nce I'd made up my mind, I worked quickly and method-
ically. I filled my hydration pack with snow and then
added some of the warm water from the skillet. I packed up a
portion of what was left of our food, leaving a ration for Dad.
I only hoped he'd be clearheaded enough to eat it. It made
sense for me to transfer more of the emergency items from
Dad's pack into mine, but again it was a balance of what I
could carry versus what I absolutely needed. I wanted to
travel lightly, but I didn't know exactly what the backcountry had in store for me.

It was still dark outside as I prepared to leave, but it's not
as if I could sleep anyway. Plus, the sooner I set off, the sooner
I could find help. Molly had been alert, following my every
movement, like she knew what I was planning. "Okay, I
know," I said. "I need to test before we go."

After a normal level reading, I had no more excuses. I
kissed my father on the head. "I love you, Dad," I said. Then
Molly and I left, and it was one of the hardest things I've ever
done. My fear whispered doubts into my ear the entire time.

"You'll never make it. You're not strong enough. Your body will fail you."

My heart screamed back, "But I have to try!"

A blast of frigid air hit me the moment I stepped outdoors. Even with all my layers, I was miserably cold. I only hoped that my body would warm with movement.

Sempre Avanti, I told myself. Always forward.

One last thing, though. I didn't have the time or energy to gather rocks, but I found enough sticks to spell out a large SOS in the snow nearby before leaving the cabin and Dad behind me.

Gliding through the snow had a much different feel than it had before. I was determined and resolute. I was driven by fear and anxiety rather than a sense of fun and adventure. But the same rules applied. I stayed on top of my hydration. And even though I was worried about running out of food, I fueled my body with nuts and dried fruit. Every so often, I checked the topographic maps and used the compass I'd pilfered from Dad's pack to be certain I was still headed in the right direction.

At first, the only light I had was the beam emitted from my headlamp. Molly dashed in and out of the glow, never straying more than a few feet from my side. But as the sun began to rise, the forest was bathed in pink, purple, and orange hues.

My fingers and toes prickled as the temperature began to rise, and my heart tingled with the awakening of hope. Difficult things always felt more possible at sunrise than in the dark of night.

My thoughts were all over the place as I skied through the backcountry alone. Even though Dad had been a quiet companion, I hadn't realized what a difference his presence had made. I'd been distracted by wanting to impress him, by keeping pace with him and relying on his knowledge and experience.

Now I was alone with my thoughts, and I felt the pressure of our well-being lying entirely on my shoulders. It felt more doable in the daylight, but it was still an enormous weight to carry along with the extra items in my pack.

I thought about how I'd brushed off Mom's hug when we'd left and how I'd been annoyed by her level of concern. I thought about how I'd ghosted Tanner and how I'd pushed him away since my diagnosis. I would've given anything for a chance to see them both again. I thought about Dad's pale face and the anguish I knew he'd been trying to hide from me as I'd dragged him to the cabin.

Something shifted inside me as my understanding of my reality changed. Something that I hadn't expected. I was every bit as aware of my diabetes and the extra needs of my body, but it took a back seat for once. It wasn't the BIG thing that defined my every waking moment. It hit me that I was so much more than my illness. I was a daughter, a friend, an athlete, a student, and today I also had to be someone brave and courageous. Nothing, not diabetes or anything else, could stand in the way of getting me and Dad out of this awful situation.

When it came time for my first insulin shot of the day, I took a deep breath. It still terrified me, but I had to do it. I removed my skis, found a comfortable spot in the snow, and got out my kit. As I went through the steps to prepare, Molly sat patiently beside me. While my glove was off, I took the opportunity to scratch behind her ear. She stared back at me appreciatively, but I think it might've done more for me than for her. "Here goes nothing, right?" It was the last I had of the long-acting insulin. It would keep at least a little insulin in my body until the following morning. My heart raced as I pressed the injection pen against my upper thigh. I didn't hesitate quite as long this time and it was over in an instant. If only all the hard things I had to accomplish that day went as smoothly.

I kept a steady pace all morning even though the terrain was way more challenging than the trails we'd skied in on. Molly could squeeze under logs and forge her own path. I couldn't. I had to pick my way around fallen trees, boulders, and uneven ground, and still manage to stay on track. Without trail blazes, it was even easier to get turned around and headed in the wrong direction.

At one point, I somehow circled back and came across my own tracks. A hard lump formed in my throat as I withdrew the compass from my coat pocket and got the map out of my bag. I thought I'd known where I was headed. Obviously, I didn't, and it's not like I had a lot of spare time. I couldn't afford to get lost.

I checked the map again and attempted to pinpoint my location. It was far from easy when all I had to look at was a bunch of wavy lines. Going off the relative flatness of the land around me and the proximity to the ridge, I took my best guess and oriented myself with the compass. As long as I kept traveling west, I should come across the highway eventually.

What I didn't consider, but really should have, was the thin blue line on the map—the line that indicated a river. The sun was high in the sky when I first heard the gurgle of rushing water. I knew at once what it was, but I didn't think it was going to be a problem. In fact, I thought it was a good thing, considering the water in my hydration pack was getting low.

The sound of the river flowing between rocks and ice was pleasant and calming. Other than the sound of my skis swooshing through the snow, I hadn't heard much of anything since I'd left Dad and the crackle of the fire. Silence is peaceful, but it can also be maddening. Especially when you're desperate to find another human being—someone, anyone, who can provide help. All morning long I'd listened for any sound of life, but the forest had been mute. I rushed toward the river and its alluring song.

It wasn't until I reached the river's edge that I realized what a problem it was going to present. Ice-cold water cascaded over boulders and snow-covered logs. It was nearly as wide as a basketball court is long. As far as I could see, there was no way across and no way around.

Molly lapped from water pooling by our feet. "Now what?" I asked. This river was every bit as breathtaking as the one we'd seen on our second day. It struck me that things could be both beautiful and dangerous. There was no question that we needed to find a way to get to the other side. But the current was fast and without a bridge . . . well, the task seemed as unlikely as me safely climbing to the top of the bluff.

I skied downstream, hoping to find an area where the river narrowed. Molly ran behind in my tracks. There was one spot where a wide log was suspended several feet above the river. It appeared promising, but beyond the log was a large boulder. I thought I might be able to drop down from the log and hop to the other side, but I wasn't confident I'd be successful.

I skied a little farther, hoping to find a better solution. Instead, I ran into thick overgrowth. What I saw just beyond took my breath away. The river funneled into fast-flowing streams, and the water seemed to touch the blue-gray sky. It rippled around boulders and then disappeared off the edge of the earth. I didn't know how far the river plunged, but from the soft roar reaching my ears, I knew I didn't want to cross anywhere near the falls.

I pivoted on my skis and returned to the log and boulder. I thought and thought and thought on it, wishing I had a better option. I was worried that even if I could make it across, Molly couldn't. I considered turning back, but I'd wasted half a day already. And the only way to more insulin, which I desperately needed, was on the other side of the river. Sempre Avanti. Always forward.

I removed my skis and pack. With the aid of straps, I was able to attach them to my backpack. Once I'd slipped it back on, I clambered up the fallen log. It was slick with frozen snow. I inched forward, then coaxed Molly to follow. "Come on, girl," I said. "Jump."

Molly made it look easy as she sprang up behind me on the log. I carefully swiveled toward the river and took a deep breath. Looking down at the running water made me dizzy. I kept my gaze at an angle—mostly ahead but also with the log in view so I wouldn't trip.

My pack and skis made me feel unbalanced, though, and I nearly lost my footing anyway as I ventured out over the river. So I dropped to my hands and knees, deciding it was best to crawl. I hugged the log as I scooted to the end of it.

The distance between the log and the boulder was greater than I'd estimated. I considered turning back again, but I knew I couldn't. I slowly and shakily rose to my feet. Then, before I could chicken out, I leaped.

I had the distance, but the boulder was slippery, and I stumbled forward. Before I fully understood what was happening, I was being swept downstream. The icy water stole my breath. I instantly felt numb. It was all I could do to keep my head above the water as I swirled, and the current slammed me into another boulder. I heard a crunch, and pain radiated through my right shoulder.

I kicked and swam, trying to escape, but the river was more powerful. It swiftly carried me away and I panicked, remembering the falls. It'd be a miracle if I could survive the cold and beating against the rocks. If I went over the edge, I was done for.

I dug deep and summoned the strength to kick harder. I reached for and grasped a branch extending from a tree. I held on for dear life, but that's all I could do. I fought the river, but I couldn't get the upper hand. I couldn't make it to land.

I wasn't sure how much longer I could hold on. Then I saw Molly running along the riverbank. My mind was starting to feel numb as well, but I felt a twinge of joy to see she'd made it safely across. When she plunged into the river, that feeling evaporated.

My heart screamed in protest. I knew, I just knew that she was going to be swept away and there was nothing I could do about it. But then, her head popped up beside me. She latched on to my pack with her teeth and started pulling.

I couldn't make it on my own, but maybe the two of us working together could. I let go of the branch and kicked and paddled with my arms with every ounce of strength I had left. We moved a tiny bit toward the bank. It was enough to get out of the current. My boots connected with the ground and then I was scrambling to my feet and stumbling forward and falling onto the shore.

Molly emerged from the river beside me. She was

dripping wet. She immediately shook the water from her fur. My teeth chattered and I shook uncontrollably. I hardly felt any relief that we'd made it out of the river alive. Because I knew that even though we were back on land, we were far from safe.

CHAPTER 20

I felt confused and disoriented, but my thoughts were clear enough to remember that hypothermia could be deadly. I needed warmth and I needed it quickly.

I removed my pack and barely registered that one of my skis had been snapped when the river slammed me into a boulder. My fingers felt clumsy and numb as I fumbled to open the zipper, dig through the pack, and remove the waterproof match case and a ziplock baggie with petroleum jelly–soaked cotton balls. I almost hadn't taken them from Dad's pack. I was sure glad I had now.

It seemed like ages before I got a fire going. Dry wood and kindling were scarce, and my fingers were trembling as I tried to strike the matches on a rock. I wasted three of them before I got a spark and transferred the flame to one of the cotton balls. It ignited quickly. Then I gently blew on the twigs surrounding it until the flames roared to life.

My coat, ski pants, and boots were all water repellent, but not enough to repel an entire river. I shivered as I stripped them off. I'd packed a base layer of clothes in a dry bag. When my pack submerged, they'd kept dry. My body shook from head to toe the entire time I was changing and for a long time after.

I strung my wet clothing over a branch and hung it near the flames. My emergency blanket had stayed mostly dry; I draped it around my shoulders. Molly snuggled close and I was grateful for her body heat. When my mind finally started to clear, I tried to tell myself I'd been lucky. I could have been bashed by the falls. I could've knocked my head on a rock and drowned. There were so many outcomes that could've been worse. But then, I glanced at my broken ski, and I didn't *feel* lucky.

The topographic map hadn't survived the tumble I'd taken into the river, either. It was completely soaked, and the ink lines blurred together. From what I could remember, I was less than halfway to the highway. In most places, the snow was more than knee-deep. It took a great deal more energy to slog through the drifts than to ski through them. Not to mention time, which I didn't have.

As I was gathering myself and my thoughts, Molly pawed at my leg. When I stopped to test, my glucose levels were off. I needed an injection. I'd taken the last of my long-acting insulin that morning, but I had five units of bolus insulin left. On skis it might've been enough to get me to the highway. Walking? There was no way.

I dropped my head in my hands. It felt like too much. It felt like there was no way out. The river blocked my way back to the cabin and I'd never make it to the highway. I'd never hated my diabetes more than I did in that moment. Sempre Avanti? Always forward? I'd been kidding myself. I wasn't a soldier. I was sick and weak and couldn't survive one day in the wilderness. I'd wanted to prove to everyone that I was still strong and capable, but that was a lie. I wasn't Dad's champion anymore. I should never have fooled myself into thinking I was.

My thoughts went to home, and I missed it madly. If I hadn't gone on this trip, I'd have been baking holiday cookies with Mom this week and going to the rec center with Tanner. My chest felt tight, and I wanted to scream.

I did scream.

I threw my head back and let out a long, hollow wail. I thought of something Dad liked to say. "If a tree falls in the forest and no one is around to hear it, does it make a sound?"

There was no one to hear my scream; did that make it any less real? I felt detached from everything, but then Molly nudged my shoulder with her head and the sensation brought me back to the present moment. She had heard me. I wasn't alone. Not totally. I thought about how if I gave up, I wouldn't be the only one affected. Dad and Molly would be, too.

More than anything I wished their fate didn't rest on my shoulders. I couldn't do it. I thought I could, but I was wrong. I stewed and grieved as the minutes went by. Then lyrics from one of Dad's favorite songs popped into my head:

Life is rough. Can't seem to get ahead,

But if I don't die trying, I'm already dead.

I'd brushed it off the dozens of times I'd heard the song playing in Dad's truck, but it made sense to me now. My situation seemed hopeless, but if I did nothing to try to change it, I might as well be dead already. I had to keep trying for my and Molly's sake, and for Dad's. I could start by taking an injection.

Once my levels were back to normal, I had more energy. It felt like a slim chance that I'd make it to the highway, but I for sure wouldn't make it if I stayed here any longer. Even though my outer layers were still a little damp, I pulled them on anyway.

I remembered something Will had written in his letters about using pine needles for insulation. It didn't sound like the softest way to add a layer of warmth, but it's not like I had many options. I cut boughs from the tree I'd hung my clothing on. I shoved them into my ski pants and the arms of my jacket. It was a little prickly, but if I positioned the clusters of needles to match the curvature of my limbs, it wasn't so bad. And Will had been right. Not only did the pine needles provide an extra layer between my damp outerwear and my base clothing, but they also seemed to be helping my body retain heat.

Once I was done stuffing myself like a straw scarecrow, I gathered my belongings and started walking. The first few feet went fine, but soon my right leg broke through the crust of hard snow and next thing I knew, I was up to my hips in it. It was a struggle to dig my way out, let alone take another step.

Molly, on the other hand, was able to stay on top of the snow and move much more quickly. She was lighter than I was, and her weight was more evenly distributed. Watching her, I remembered something else Will had written about— weaving pine branches together to make snowshoes.

Was it possible? Could I build something to help me stay on top of the drifts the way Molly did? I doubted it. I didn't have army training, and it's not like Will had left step-by-step instructions. Besides, I was in a hurry and just wanted to get going. I almost pushed forward through the deep snow, knowing I'd be exhausted before I'd made it the length of a football field, let alone to the highway, but Dad's voice popped into my head: "Set yourself up for success."

I looked around. I was in the same environment Will had been in. Nature provided an abundance of sticks, branches, and clusters of pine needles, but I'd need something to strap them to my boots . . .

I was glad I still had the paracord bracelet Tanner had made for me and hadn't used it for Dad's splint. A pang of sadness washed over me as I undid the clasp and started unweaving it, row by row. I missed my friend so much. I said a quick prayer that this would get me back to him.

I hastily gathered more boughs of needles. Then, using my pocketknife, I cut a small piece of paracord. I laid one of the limbs against the sole of my boot while wrapping the cord around it and adding a knot on top.

When I tested it out, my heel sank in the snow and the needles worked their way forward, out of the ligature. I let out a grunt of frustration before giving it another shot. This time I used two boughs of needles, but they slipped, one to each side of my foot, when I tried to walk. Another design failure.

At that point, I'd spent too much time at it to give up. Plus, I could see the potential. The branches were catching on the snow before jiggling free and letting my foot sink. There had to be a way to secure the needles and keep everything in place. If I could stay on top of the branches somehow, I could stay on top of the snow. I just needed to get creative.

Through trial and error—I don't know how many prototypes I went through—my work evolved. I'd add a stick here and a branch there until, finally, I tried bending one of the longest branches into an oval and then tied the two ends together. I selected a few of the stronger branches to crisscross over the oval, then I secured them with paracord as well. Next, I wove some of the remaining sticks through the lattice I'd created before adding the clusters of pine needles to fill in the open spaces.

When I tried it out, and everything stayed together and kept my foot elevated on the snow, well, it was one of the proudest moments of my life, and only Molly was there to witness it. I smiled and squealed, "Yes," and she danced around me in delight. I knew she didn't know why I was so happy; she was just thrilled that I was. That was one of the things I loved the most about her. I wrapped my arms around her neck and buried my head in her fur before I set about making another snowshoe to match. Ten minutes later, I was finished. They weren't as neat and tidy as I would've liked, but they were sturdy and they'd support my weight.

It took all the paracord I had left to tie them onto my boots. They looked ridiculous—like prickly, green yeti feet. But they did the trick. They kept me from falling knee-deep into the snow with every step I took.

Molly sniffed the pine needles. "Remind me to thank Tanner when we make it out of here, okay?" Molly wagged her tail. *When*, not if. I knew I had to stay optimistic.

My pine needle snowshoes were nowhere near as smooth as my skis had been. It took more effort, but I made steady progress as I shuffled through the snow. I carried on for hours, checking my compass often to keep me headed west, and rationing my trail food. As I went, the sun dipped lower and lower in the sky. I had no way of knowing if I had one more mile to go, or ten. A nagging voice in my head doubted I was even headed in the right direction. What if I was traveling deeper and deeper into the wilderness instead of closer to civilization?

By then, the lift the successful construction of the snowshoes had given me was fully evaporated. I could feel the temperature dropping along with the sun. My fingers and toes tingled, my legs ached from walking, and the pack on my back felt like it weighed a ton. When I thought about my fear and misery, it made things worse. So I tried to focus on the things I enjoyed. The things I told myself I wouldn't take for granted ever again if I made it out of here alive.

Pulling warm, clean clothes from the dryer. My mom's beef and barley soup. Riding my bike after dark on a summer night. Scoring the winning point. Wrapping myself in the softest blanket and snuggling with Molly as I read a book. Laughing with my friends.

For every reason I had to stop, I had dozens more to keep going.

I took the last of the rapid-acting insulin right before eating what little charcuterie I'd salvaged from Dad's pack. It was too cold to stay still for long, so I ate most of my food standing up. I savored a dried apricot, sucking every bit of sweetness from it. Then I gave Molly some water and fed her a scoop of dried dog food from her pack. I knew I could eat some of her food to survive if I needed to, but I wasn't that desperate. *Yet*.

As soon as we'd finished, I dug out my headlamp and we started walking again. I likely had eight to ten hours before my body used up all the insulin from my last, long-acting injection. My muscles felt heavy with exhaustion, but I had no choice but to keep moving forward. Step by step. Every tree, every snowbank started looking the same. It seemed there was no end to any of it. Not to the cold or the distance, the worry or the loneliness. I thought things couldn't possibly get any worse. And then they did.

CHAPTER 21

Molly froze in her tracks. She bared her teeth and growled a low, threatening rumble. My skin prickled and a wave of foreboding washed over me. "What is it?" I could sense there was something in the woods—something avoiding the light from my lamp. I heard a rustle. I swiveled my head in the direction of the sound and caught a wavering branch. Then another. A form moved quickly in my peripheral vision. I wheeled again and caught a murky glance of a strong, menacing shape before it stole back into the woods and the night.

My chin trembled and I clutched my stomach, as if hugging myself could somehow protect me from the lurking beast. Where had it gone? The only thing more terrifying than catching sight of the frightful creature was knowing it was there, but not knowing exactly where it was hiding, waiting to pounce. I whipped my head around to catch another glimpse. There was more movement, but by the time I shined the beam on where I thought the noise was coming from, whatever it was had gone.

Shadows stretched long and dark on the snow, and my

chest was tight with fear. My feet were plastered to the ground. Then, time stood still as a large gray wolf slowly stepped out of the forest. His light-colored, fluffy fur seemed at odds with the dark gleam in his eerily yellow eyes. He dwarfed Molly in size, and as he crept forward with his sharp, white teeth exposed, his glare was trained on my dog. Her hackles shot up. To her credit, though, she wasn't paralyzed with fear the way I was. She snarled and growled once more.

I couldn't breathe. I still couldn't move a muscle. All I could do was stand there with my eyes bulging as Molly stepped forward and she and the wolf began circling each other. Clearly, they were sizing each other up, but there was no question in my mind which of the canines was more powerful. My stomach roiled as the wolf, no doubt, came to the same conclusion I had and sprang at Molly. I watched in pure horror as the wolf lurched for my dog and she rose on her hind legs in defense. Their bodies entangled. There was a blur of black and gray fur, and then . . .

The winner emerged with his mouth wrapped tightly around Molly's neck.

"Nooo!" I screamed at the same time Molly yelped and twisted free. She turned her gaze toward me for a brief moment before darting away. The wolf chased after her and then they were both gone—disappearing in the darkness beyond my beam of light.

It all happened so suddenly. From somewhere deep in my gut, a whimpering moan rose and escaped my lips. The noise was full of sorrow and anguish. It was so animallike that I almost didn't recognize it as my own.

I didn't care. I was frantic. How could I help her? Thoughts swirled in my head as rapidly as panic drummed, *LUP-DUP, LUP-DUP, LUP-DUP*, against my rib cage. The nightmare replayed on a loop inside my head. Could I have stopped it from happening? If I'd had Molly on her leash, or if I'd charged the wolf when he attacked, would things have gone differently?

I knew she'd run off because she was trying to protect me. She was leading the danger away. That knowledge didn't stop my heart from breaking, though. I opened my mouth again and this time, I screamed Molly's name.

A wolf howled in the distance.

The smart thing would be to flee—put as much distance as I could between me and the wolf pack. Instead, without hesitation, I started following the tracks. I could see five to ten feet in front of me in a cone of light as I kept my headlamp pointed at the snow. At first, there was a small amount of distance between Molly's prints and the much larger ones.

Then the distance closed, and the snow was stamped down in an area as though the two had tussled. The sight of three small, dark red drops of blood in the snow made my stomach clench.

Still, the tracks continued on the other side. Molly wasn't seriously hurt. Not yet. I couldn't run with my rudimentary snowshoes, and it was hopeless to think I'd ever be able to catch them, but I plowed forward anyway.

I don't know how long I followed the tracks. I followed them until time had no meaning and the terrain grew rugged. The footprints led to rocky, uneven ground and then just stopped. The incline was great enough that even if I could see the tracks, I couldn't follow.

I pulled down my balaclava and cupped my hands around my mouth. "Molly!" I called. "Molly!"

As I flashed my light up the slope, I scanned for movement. I wanted so badly to see her dark form appear in front of me. She and the wolf had covered the ground far quicker than I was capable of with my awkward pine needle steps. For all I knew, they were on the opposite side of the mountain already.

Nonetheless, I waited and called for my dog until my lips were chapped from the frigid air and my voice was all but gone.

I lost hours searching for Molly. Hours I didn't have. I

was so cold and beaten down, and now I truly was alone. I collapsed in the snow. The only way out of this was for me to keep going, but I couldn't get back to my feet. I couldn't summon the strength to do anything but sit there.

All the uncertainty felt like it was shackling me to the ground. First Dad, now Molly. I didn't know if any of us would make it out of this alive. Molly had been easy to love since day one. She'd been trained to stay by my side, but it had never felt like her training was the reason she was so attentive. It felt like she wanted to be there, and I'd wanted her there, too. Losing her felt like losing a part of myself.

Once again, I found my thoughts jumping around to all those closest to me. The quiet stillness of my surroundings seemed to amplify my heartache. I hoped Dad wasn't suffering too much. I hoped he understood why I had to leave. I wondered what Mom was doing at this moment—winding down for bed, most likely. She liked to watch old movies when Dad and I were busy with other things. I pictured her curled up on the couch with a blanket and a cup of chamomile tea and the glow from the TV illuminating her face.

Why hadn't I told her I loved her the last time we talked on the phone? I'd been annoyed because she was lecturing me about my relationship with Tanner. I was sick of how she was always so worried about me, but that didn't excuse the way I'd treated her. Was she worried now? Did she have some sort of Mom-sense that would tell her I was in actual trouble? Even if she did, I was miles away from where I was supposed to be. It wasn't just when we talked on the phone; I'd also brushed her off the morning we left. I didn't want my last words to her to be a bristly "Yeah, okay, see ya."

I'd wasted time worrying I'd say the wrong thing around Tanner. Instead of opening up, I'd let things become strange between us. I couldn't even remember the last words I'd spoken to him. If I made it out of this, I promised myself I would fix it somehow. All of it.

It was getting harder and harder to carry on, but what choice did I have? Molly had led the wolves away so that I'd be safe. I owed it to her to keep going. There was no time for mourning or regret now. Even without testing, I could tell I was low. So I popped four sugar cubes into my mouth and checked my compass. Then I shakily rose to my feet and started putting one foot in front of the other again.

CHAPTER 22

The forest seemed so much darker without Molly by my side. The loudest noise was the crunch of snow beneath my feet. But every branch quivering in the wind, every whisper, swish, or crackle the woods made, sent my heart racing with terror. Wolves traveled in a pack. I'd only seen one, but the others had to be close by.

I was so caught up in my fear that when I came to a treeless area, my only thought was relief. Out in the open, a wolf couldn't catch me by surprise.

I trekked across the snow, leaning slightly to counteract the downward slope. It wasn't until I heard a loud *whumpf* that I realized my mistake. Wolves were not the only danger I faced. They weren't even the biggest one.

I froze in place as a half-inch crack appeared in the snow a few feet above where I was standing. The noise had been a warning. The snow I was on was unstable. Fresh powder on top of ice. It could slide at any moment.

Adrenaline flushed my system—ten times stronger than any rush I'd felt in a high-stakes game. Every instinct I had told me to run. But I knew running was the wrong move. It would, no doubt, trigger a full-on avalanche.

I stood deathly still, scared to even breathe. If I didn't move, maybe the world wouldn't slip out from under me. The problem was, I couldn't stay like that forever.

While the minutes ticked by, I grew colder and stiffer. When nothing happened, though, I also grew bolder. If I could make it above the crack, the snow might be more compacted and less likely to break away. I knew the snowshoes distributed some of my weight, but not enough. I carefully, deliberately lowered myself to my hands and knees. Then at a pace so slow I was barely moving, I crawled up the hill. When I was well above the crack, I rose to my feet and took swift, gentle steps until I'd cleared the area.

Once I was well beyond the unstable slope, I stopped to rest. I had no choice. I'd filled my hydration pack at the river, but it was bone dry again. Not to mention that I felt weak and shaky and had spent way too long in the cold without any sleep. I knew I couldn't afford to be careless. I had to pay attention to my surroundings. Yet I'd nearly triggered an avalanche because I hadn't been thinking clearly enough to notice the warning signs. Next time, I might not be so fortunate.

Using a flat, hollow log, I dug a small cave into the side of a snowbank. I removed my pine needle snowshoes. Without them, the hole was barely large enough for me to crawl inside. Just outside the shelter, I used my matches and some more of the petroleum jelly–soaked cotton balls to light a fire.

Since I didn't have a pot or even a skillet, I took the hydration pack out of my bag, filled it with snow, and then hung it from a stick near the fire. I was out of food. My heart panged for Molly when I realized that eating dog food wasn't even an option now.

I missed Molly. I missed my family and friends. I missed everyone on the face of the planet. I couldn't remember how many hours it had been since I'd slept. The darkness of the night seemed to seep into the corners of my mind. I'd been through so much and I didn't know how much more I could bear. The fire warmed my toes and my fingers, but it couldn't reach the frozen grip of despair that had wrapped around my heart.

After a while, I dozed off. I dreamt I was back in the icy river, tumbling out of control. I awoke to the eerie cry of a wolf. I didn't know if it was real or part of my dream. Either way, I was shivering and didn't feel at all rested. I didn't want to move, but I knew I had to get up while I still could. After crawling out of the cave, I stretched my tired muscles. The fire had all but burned out while I slept. At least the ice in my hydration pack was almost entirely melted. I sipped a small amount from the hose before dousing the embers with snow.

I hated how sluggish I felt. I blamed my diabetes. I thought, if only I was the same person I'd been before, this wouldn't be so hard. I'd been strong and energetic. I'd craved physical challenges, hadn't I? Now even tying the snowshoes back on my feet exhausted me. I was scared my body would shut down—that because of my illness, I'd never make it. It wasn't fair. In the days and weeks after my diagnosis, it was weird to be around people laughing and going on with their lives like nothing had changed. For them, nothing had. But even though I looked normal on the outside, my life had been turned upside down.

Thinking about it made me angry all over again. Weirdly, my anger seemed to help. At least, more than despair did. It gave me the added umph I needed to overcome my weariness. I started moving again and I didn't stop. I took step after step after step. I trudged through the snow, not thinking, not feeling—just moving.

The darkness seemed endless in the moonless night. There was no mistaking it this time—the sound of wolves' howling echoed in the distance. I was frozen, tired, hungry, and numb. But I kept going.

Until I stumbled.

A branch on my snowshoe caught on a rock. I catapulted forward, throwing my arms out to catch myself. My elbows landed on a hard patch of snow. I bounced and skidded to a stop on my side, my head shaken from the impact.

A hot tear slid down my cheek. I wasn't hurt. Not really. I was just tired of being knocked down. Every time I thought I might have a chance, something else went wrong. What was the point? I wanted to come on this trip to prove to Dad that I was still the champion he'd always been so proud of. But the truth of the matter was, I wasn't. My body was weak. I feared I didn't have the same spirit and fire anymore. I'd given it my all, and the backcountry had beaten me. That's all there was to it.

I didn't have the willpower or the energy to lift myself up again. It was easier to stop fighting. I told myself that even if I didn't make it, someone would find Dad eventually. He had food. He had a decent chance of surviving until help arrived.

I was so very cold, and tired. My cheek ached where it was pressed against small, sharp crystals of ice. I wondered which would kill me first, the diabetes or hypothermia. Either way, I hoped it wouldn't hurt. I hoped it would feel like falling asleep.

I tried to stay alert. But eventually, I couldn't help but close my eyes and wait for the end to come.

CHAPTER 23

I dreamt Molly was pawing at my leg. Imagining her there with me was comforting. "Mmmmm," I moaned. My voice was hoarse, and my throat felt like sandpaper. When I felt another, harder nudge, I opened my eyes.

A dark form hovered above me. I was engulfed by fear, and my heart beat wildly within my chest.

The wolves had found me.

But then the form drew close to my face and sweet brown eyes peered into mine. I fought through the confusion clouding my mind. Not a wolf, and I hadn't been dreaming.

Molly! I thought I'd never see her again. I reached my gloved hand up to gently stroke behind her ear. She yelped. Her fur was matted with blood close to where I'd petted her. "Oh, Molly."

The wolves could've hurt her far worse, but my heart still ached seeing she was in pain. She dropped to the snow beside me, and I draped my arm across her back. Up close, I could see that the wound wasn't too deep.

Careful to avoid her wound, I nuzzled my head in her soft, silky fur. She burrowed deeper against the curvature of my body, leaving no space between us. The look in her eye told me she'd missed me as much as I'd missed her.

She'd be all right. Wouldn't she? What would happen to her after I . . . I couldn't finish that thought. Would she be able to find food and survive in the wilderness, or would she find her way back to civilization? Would she be reconnected with my parents?

What if the wolves found her again?

I don't know if it was the warmth from her body or the relief of no longer being utterly alone, but I started to feel more alert. There was a rim of pinkish orange beneath the darkened sky. It was almost morning.

I didn't want to die. I didn't want Molly to have to survive on her own.

It wasn't like me to give up, not without a fight. What had Dad said? Something about him being glad I got my mom's grit and determination. I thought that might be more important than being fast or strong or agile. My body had changed, but my heart hadn't.

If the backcountry took me, I wasn't going to be lying down.

Ignoring my body's protests, I dragged myself to my feet.

Molly sprang up beside me. I didn't have to check my compass—I could orient myself using the sun. I turned my back on the glow breaking through the trees and started walking. My mind returned to the last letter I'd read before leaving Dad behind in the cabin.

May 2nd, 1945

Dear Mother and Father,

You must have been so worried when the letters stopped coming. I assume you received the telegram stating that I'd been wounded. Know that I would've written if it wasn't for the shrapnel in my right arm, and the doctor's orders to keep it immobilized. Rest assured that I am being well fed and well treated, that I'm healing quickly, and will soon be back to my normal self.

So much has happened since we took the Vista Ridge. We proved quite skillful at driving back the enemy. We went house to house, facing snipers and machine gun fire. The bombardment was nearly constant, not to mention costly. I shudder to think of all the casualties. As for myself, I was hit while my platoon was moving across a gulley in a wooded area.

Now, as I write this, the radio beside my hospital bed is blasting news that the German Army in Italy has surrendered to the Allies. Meanwhile the war rages on in northern Europe. Still, I am filled with hope. If we can beat the Nazis here in this wretched terrain, we can beat them anywhere.

Love always,

Will

As far as I could tell, Will had never wavered in his bravery. He'd had low moments. He'd lost friends, and he'd been wounded, but he'd never succumbed, never given up the fight. He'd held on to the hope that he and his fellow snow soldiers would do the impossible, and they had. It struck me that the key to courage was never letting hope die—a mammoth battle in itself. Still, it was a goal I could reach for. With every difficult step I took, I told myself I was getting closer and closer to the highway. Closer to help, and to being reunited with the people I loved.

The landscape dipped in front of me, which would have made skiing a breeze but was more difficult to traverse in my pine needle snowshoes. I had to brace myself with every step to keep from falling. I wished I was walking toward the sunrise, instead of away from it. I didn't feel like I could take another step forward into the darkness. But then the rays of early morning light rose over the highest peak and cut through the forest, illuminating my path.

Frost-covered branches glistened like diamonds, and in the distance, I could just make out a road snaking through the trees. I nearly fell to my knees. "Thank you, God," I whispered. The headlights on a few cars shined brighter than the dawn. Rescue seemed all at once so close and yet so far when each step seemed to take more energy than I had left inside me.

At least my objective was now in view. I set my sights on the highway and willed myself to keep going. I felt oddly disconnected from everything around me. Nothing mattered other than making it to the road. It felt like walking through a dream. I was aware of Molly keeping pace beside me, but only dimly. My head was so fuzzy that I could hardly remember why I needed to make it to the highway. I only knew that it was important.

Little by little, I made progress. The road grew from a line to a wide black streak winding through the snow. My thoughts were woolly. I so badly wanted to lie down and sleep. Instead, I carried on in a trance until at last, one snowshoe scuffed against the freshly plowed asphalt.

A red blur appeared in my peripheral vision. It was speeding toward me. I waved my arms and then collapsed on the side of the road.

CHAPTER 24

I don't remember the car ride. I know I was picked up by an older, retired couple. They were on their way to their second home when they saw me step out of the forest. No cell service meant calling 911 wasn't immediately possible. Between the two of them, they were able to lift me into their SUV.

Molly wouldn't leave my side. I was told that she jumped right into the back seat without any coaxing. The Johnsons drove me to the nearest town. Once they had service, they called an ambulance. They reached my mom by calling the number on Molly's tag.

As the paramedic attended to me in the ambulance, I managed to tell her about Dad. Everything after that was blurry and déjà vu–ish. It was my second time riding in an ambulance in the past year. This time, instead of fear and confusion, I felt an overwhelming sense of relief.

The paramedic was a young woman with kind eyes and curly hair pulled into a ponytail at the nape of her neck. She allowed Molly to ride with us and even tended to the small wound on her neck where she'd been attacked by the wolf. Then, when we got to the hospital, she spoke to the attendants and made sure Molly could accompany me to my room as well.

Mom arrived later in sweatpants and looking totally bedraggled. She'd left the house within minutes of the Johnsons' phone call and had driven straight to the hospital. Molly started wagging her tail moments before the door opened. As soon as it did, Mom ran to my bedside and threw her arms around me. "You had me so worried!"

I hugged her back. Hard. Then with my throat tight, I said, "Dad?"

Mom nodded and tears pooled in her eyes. "They found him, thanks to you. He was airlifted in a helicopter and is being seen by an ER doctor now. We should be able to visit him soon. You were so brave."

I'd thought this experience would make Mom worry about me even more. So what she said next surprised me. "All I could think about on the drive here is what it must've been like for you to be out there on your own. I can't imagine what you must've gone through. I don't know that I would've survived it."

Mom gave me a sad, soft smile before continuing. "I got so scared when we found out you had diabetes, but you're far more capable of taking care of yourself than I've ever given you credit for. I'm so proud of you."

I felt a surge of joy, and my own smile spread wide across my face. "The extra sugar cubes were a good idea," I said. "Oh, and I gave myself shots."

"I bet you did." Mom sat down on the edge of my bed. "I want to hear all about it."

Mom focused her attention on me while I shared every detail, but after I was through, she kept glancing at the time on her phone. I knew she was anxious for news about Dad. It was nice to see her showing so much concern for his well-being.

Minutes felt like hours, but at last, a nurse came to update us on Dad's condition. He was stable, conscious, and asking for us. Mom breathed an enormous sigh of relief. But the thing was, I was nervous to face Dad. Something I hadn't allowed myself to think about while we were both in mortal danger was that I'd talked him out of turning back. If we'd cut the trip short, the way he'd wanted, we wouldn't have gotten caught in the storm, and neither of us would be in the hospital right now.

What if, now that he was thinking clearly, he blamed me for what had happened? More than anything, I'd wanted our backcountry adventure to bring us closer together. But he might resent the fact that I'd pressed so hard for something that wound up causing him such extreme pain. We'd survived, but I still worried that this would mean the end of any sort of meaningful relationship with my dad.

I hung back while we entered Dad's room. Mom, on the other hand, rushed to the side of his bed where his bad leg was propped up. The ordeal had only lasted a few days, but his cheeks were sunken in as if he hadn't eaten for weeks. His eyes were glassy, and his skin was pale. Still, the warm smile on his face gave me hope. Even if it was directed at Mom.

All things considered, he seemed in pretty good spirits when he opened his mouth to speak. "The doctor said I'll need surgery and it's going to take some time to heal. But she was impressed with how the bones were set in the field." He turned his gaze toward me. "She said to pass along her compliments to our budding first responder."

That gave me a much-needed boost of confidence, and I stepped closer to his bed.

"I'll see if I can catch her," Mom said. "I'd like to know what we're in for, recovery-wise." She kissed Dad on the forehead before leaving the room.

He watched her go, his eyes full of affection. I hadn't seen him look at Mom that way for a very long time, and a lingering sheet of ice melted from my heart.

After she was gone, Dad's smile turned playfully crooked. "Don't think I'll be skiing again this season. I can't imagine that you're too anxious to get back out there, either. Not after what you went through."

All too aware of his bad leg, I warily sat down on the side of his hospital bed. "Actually," I said, "I was hoping I could go back sometime soon. There's something I want to do . . ."

To be honest, I didn't know if I was still trying to impress him. My life had been turned upside down again. Who could blame me for being bewildered? I only knew that I longed to connect with Dad, and that meant being open about my feelings. As I told him about how I'd wanted to prove myself to him, then how I'd learned about Will and drawn strength from the snow soldier's courage, and finally laid out my plans to return to the backcountry, Dad remained silent. He studied my face.

Before all this, Dad had been a treasure trove of idioms and inspirational phrases. *Break a leg. Take the bull by the horns. Keep on keepin' on.* Usually, he had good advice, but he hardly ever said anything . . . real.

I think what we'd been through had made us both more reflective.

No doubt, before all this, he would've said something

about how proud he was of me for getting back in the game, or saddle, or whatever. Instead, he smiled wistfully. "You know I love you, don't you?"

"So you aren't mad at me for making us go on? You don't blame me for that?" I nodded at his casted leg.

He didn't hesitate a millisecond. "Of course not! Pain is part of life. What doesn't kill you makes you stronger, right?" There was the Dad I knew and loved. Still, I really wanted to hear him speak from the heart, not spout off clichés.

My smile faltered, just a little. But for once, Dad actually picked up on it. He held my gaze. "Look, you don't have to earn my love. You don't have to do anything but be you. I love you. I'm proud of you. I think you're amazing. And that's never going to change."

A hard lump formed in my throat. He sounded like he meant it, but . . . "Then why aren't you ever around?" I said boldly. It was a question I'd wanted to ask him for years, but I'd never had the courage until now.

Dad winced and I had to check to be sure I hadn't accidentally bumped his bad leg. Turns out, it was his heart that was hurting. "When I came to at the cabin and you weren't there . . ." He choked up. "I did a lot of thinking. I'm so sorry, Em. I can't get all the time I missed with you back, can I? I thought I was doing what was best for you and your

mother. I thought I was giving you everything you needed."
He dropped his head. "I was wrong."

It was a lot to take in. I'd never heard my dad apologize
for anything. I'd felt like his love had been dependent on how
well I performed on the court, how many points I scored,
how fast I ran. Maybe I'd been wrong, too.

The realization made me question everything. When
we'd set out on our trip, my focus had been entirely on
showing him I could still compete at the top level. I thought
getting him to sponsor my competitive volleyball team was
the most important thing in the world. Ever since the storm,
I'd hardly thought about it. Still, I wanted to know where
things stood. "Are you going to sponsor the Impalers again?"
I asked. "Or do you think I'm done playing competitive
sports?"

He raised his chin. "Honestly, Em, I think you can do
anything you set your mind to. If you want to play for the
Impalers, I'll support you one hundred percent. You've just
been through so much. I knew if I sponsored the team, you'd
feel like you had to keep playing, no matter what. I didn't
want to force you if your heart isn't in it anymore. I guess I
didn't make that clear, though, did I?"

Not at all, I thought at the same time I shrugged. Was my
heart still in it? The thing was, I'd never felt like I'd had an

option before. There were other things I loved doing, skiing for one. I'd always felt I'd be letting Dad down if I wasn't a star athlete. But volleyball took up a great deal of my time. If I was going to commit, I wanted to be sure I was playing for the right reasons from now on. "I want to think about it, okay? Coach Vega won't call for another week or so . . . and the season won't start for another month."

"Of course," Dad said. "If you decide to play, I'll sponsor the team. Heck, even if you don't, I'll still sponsor the team. It's good advertising, you know."

I smiled. "Thanks, Dad." It felt like a huge weight had been lifted. If I didn't play next season, it wouldn't be because I wasn't capable—not in Dad's eyes or my own. And I felt even freer to choose, knowing my teammates would be supported whether I played or not.

I sprang forward for a giant hug. I'd embraced him after hundreds of wins, but this hug was by far the sweetest.

May 8th, 1945

Dearest Family,

It is over. Hitler is dead and the Germans have signed an unconditional surrender to the Allies. How can I describe this feeling? It is

more than relief, more than joy, more than
sadness for my friends who did not live to see
this day. It is all the emotions rolled into one.
My arm is nearly healed and there is nothing
I desire more than to use it to draw my loved
ones close. Yet, as victory celebrations ring
out across the world, I find myself longing
not for the cheer of crowds, but for the peace
and solitude of the mountains that in a
roundabout way brought me here. Therefore,
after we are reunited, do not be alarmed if I
head straight for the wilderness. It is a call I
cannot ignore.

Forever yours,

Will

The following weekend, I was back at the trailhead. This
time, it was Tanner putting skins on his skis beside me
instead of Dad. "I can't believe your mom is okay with this,"
he said after she drove off.

We were only going to the first hut and returning, all in
one day. Still, we would be gone for hours with limited
communication. "It took some convincing," I admitted. "But

she's really lightened up. Also, if we don't make it back by sundown, she's calling in the National Guard." I was joking, of course, but I could tell it didn't sit well with my best friend.

As he dipped his head, I caught a glance of his puffed-out cheeks and scrunched brow. He wasn't as experienced a skier as I was, and I knew he was nervous.

"Don't worry," I said. "You're going to love it." Molly wagged her tail and brushed against his leg as if to confirm my statement.

Tanner petted her back and then met my eyes. His grin was sheepish. Not many things scared him, and I knew he was embarrassed by his fear.

"It's okay," I said. "If you're not at least a little bit frightened, you probably shouldn't be out here. Being full of yourself on the court is one thing. In the wilderness, it'll get you killed."

He nodded and I could sense him relaxing. "I'm glad you asked me to come," he said. He sounded like he meant it, too.

As we started off on our trek to the Summit hut, I tried explaining to Tanner why I'd been acting so distant. "When Dad and I went on our trip, there was this other traveler that we met. She treated me differently when she found out I had diabetes. Like I was some sort of specimen. And, honestly, you treated me differently, too. Not like that woman, Chloe, but still . . . you went easier on me when we played basketball. I thought the more I talked about it, the worse it would get. I'm not fragile. I'm still the same person I've always been." As it left my mouth, I realized that my last statement wasn't exactly true. I wasn't the same. I was stronger. Maybe not physically, but I could handle hard things. Things that I wasn't sure I could have handled before.

"I know you're not fragile," Tanner said. He stopped to catch his breath, so Molly and I stopped, too. "But I thought it would be extra dangerous for you out here because of your diabetes."

"Yeah," I said. "That's true." I paused, mulling it over. "At the same time, I think my diabetes is part of the reason I survived."

"Really?"

"It made it more difficult, for sure, but not giving up was half the battle. And since I'd already been through something so tough, I knew how to keep going forward even when things went wrong." *Sempre Avanti*, I thought, and smiled to myself.

It was another bluebird day and we'd ditched our balaclavas. I watched as a sly grin spread across Tanner's face. "So you're saying I've got a good ski buddy in case we run into trouble."

I grinned back. "More than good."

"We'll see about that," Tanner said as he abruptly shot off in the lead. Still, it wasn't long before Molly and I were passing him by.

When we stopped for me to check my levels, and I needed a shot, I explained to Tanner everything I was doing. "Even though I'm pretty comfortable with the tools now, I need people I trust around me in case I miss the warning signs, or something doesn't go as planned. Do you think . . . Are you . . . Um . . ." I stumbled on my words, trying not to sound stupid or corny as I asked for his help.

"Hey," he said quietly. "I'm on your team. Always have been. Always will be."

Guess I shouldn't have worried about sounding corny. "Thanks," I said, then I threw a snowball at him before speeding off. "Race you there!"

Because our trip got derailed, I'd never had the opportunity to return the book I borrowed to Summit Hut. Dad said we could mail it back to the Tenth Mountain Division and they'd take care of it. But I wanted the satisfaction of placing it back on the bookshelf myself. I wanted to be sure that another lucky reader would be able to follow Will's journey to victory.

At my first appointment, Dr. Morlock said everyone has

their own battle to fight and that diabetes is mine. I sort of tuned him out the way I tune out Dad whenever he starts in with the motivational talk. You can only hear that you have to give something 110 percent so many times before it starts to lose some meaning. I guess I thought, *Yeah right, you just told me I'll have diabetes for the rest of my life, so it's not a battle I can win.*

I understood better now what he meant. Victory comes in all different shapes and forms. It doesn't always mean that you defeat your opponent, like in a volleyball match or the Nazis surrendering to the Allies. Sometimes victory means that you stop letting something have power over you. Maybe Dad was right, that I'd always had grit. But what the back-country taught me was that even though I had diabetes, it didn't have me.

ACKNOWLEDGMENTS

I am humbled to have the continued support of all the wonderful people at Scholastic.

My editor, Mallory Kass, is unparalleled. She astonishes me time after time with her brilliance, kindness, and creativity.

Many thanks to Rachel Jaffe for her insightful and informative feedback. This book is better because of it.

It is an honor to work with my lovely agent, Ginger Knowlton. I'd be lost without her advice.

My life has been greatly blessed with dear friends and the finest family. I love you all.

Lastly, my deepest thanks to God, who strengthens me and gives me hope.

ABOUT THE AUTHOR

Jenny Goebel is the author of *Grave Images*, The 39 Clues: *Mission Hurricane*, *Fortune Falls*, *Out of My Shell*, *Alpaca My Bags,* and *Pigture Perfect*. She lives in Denver with her husband and three sons. She can be found online at jennygoebel.com.